사막의　장미꽃

사막의 장미석

초판 1쇄 | 2014년 3월 20일 발행

지은이 | 신기섭 펴낸곳 | 해누리 고문 | 이동진 펴낸이 | 김진용
편집주간 | 조종순 디자인 | 신나미 표지 디자인 | 류명식
마케팅 | 김진용·유재영
등록 | 1998년 9월 9일(제16-1732호)
등록 변경 | 2013년 12월 9일(제2002-000398호)
주소 | 121-251 서울시 마포구 성미산로 60(성산동, 성진빌딩)
전화 | (02)335-0414 팩스 | (02)335-0416
E-mail | haenuri0414@naver.com

ⓒ 신기섭, 2014

ISBN 978-89-6226-041-0 (03810)

Rose Stone in Arabian Sand

First Publication | March 20, 2014

Author | Shin Kee Sup
Translator | Lee Dong Jin
Publisher | Kim Jin Yong
Editor | Cho Jong Soon
Design | Shin Na Mi
Cover Design | Ryu Myung Shik

Registration | Sep 9, 1998(No.16-1732)
Revision | Dec 9, 2013

Address | 121-251 Sungmisan-ro 60, Mapo-gu, Seoul
          (Sungson-dong Sungjin Bldg)
Tel | 82-2-335-0414 Fax | 82-2-335-0416
E-mail | haenuri0414@naver.com

ⓒ Shin Kee Sup 2014

Shin Kee Sup English Korean Poetry Publication
신기섭 영한시집

사막의 장미석

Rose
Stone
in
Arabian
Sand

신기섭 지음
이동진 옮김

해누리

Contents

Part Three   The Sea

Part Four Exotic Poems / Korean Poems

When I made my debut as a poet in 《Shimsang》, a monthly magazine founded by the famous poet Mok-wol Park, I wrote that, "my contribution, as one of Korea's many poets, to our culture & Korean literature would be to broaden the themes of Korean poetry to the wider world."

30 years have passed since I first mentioned those words, and as I prepare to publish my English-Korean poetry book 《*Rose Stone in Arabian Sand*》, the fact that these initial remarks have carried me through my many experiences in the Middle East, Indonesia and other Islamic countries is deeply humbling.

The members of my family have a unique history of being frontiers of overseas advancement. My father, Chairman Shin Kyo-hwan, was conscripted while studying abroad at Tokyo Imperial University and experienced the Second World War as a student-soldier in Ambon Island, Indonesia. Having narrowly escaped from death, he whole-heartedly embraced August 15th, 1945, the day of Korea's liberation from Japanese colonial rule. When Korea faced a severe unemployment crisis in the 1960s, he advocated his vision for the future of Korean people by saying that "the only way for us to survive and prosper is to venture overseas."

1983년 목월선생님이 창간한 〈심상〉지를 통해 등단하면서
"한국의 수많은 시인들 가운데 내가 기여할 수 있는 부분은
한국시의 소재의 폭을 세계로 넓히는 것이다." 라는 소감을 피
력한 바 있다. 그러한 초심이 30년이 지나 중동, 인도네시아
등 이슬람국가의 소재를 중심으로 한 영한시집《Rose Stone
in Arabian Sand》를 발간하는 계기가 되어 감회가 새롭다.

우리 집안은 '해외개척의 선구자' 라는 특이한 내력이 있다.
아버님 신교환(辛敎煥)회장은 일제시대 동경제대 유학 중 학병
으로 차출되어 인도네시아 암본섬에서 '2차 세계대전' 을 겪
으며 구사일생으로 살아나 1945년 8.15 해방을 맞이하였다.

1960년대 암울한 실업난에 시달리던 한국에서 "해외개척만
이 살 길이다" 며 한민족이 나아가야 할 미래비전을 역설하시
다가 스스로 실천의 주체가 되어 어머님 송복순(宋福順)여사과
함께 자원의 나라 인도네시아로 진출해, 온갖 역경을 딛고 원
목개발을 성공시킨 사업가로서 입지를 다졌다. 2대 인도네시
아 한인회장으로 인도네시아 지도부, 서민층을 가리지 않고

He lived pursuing this great vision and settled in Indonesia, a country of abundant natural resources, with my mother Song Bok-soon. After overcoming innumerable hardships, he found success in the business of timber development and plywood manufacturing. He was elected as the second Chairman of Koreans' Association in Indonesia, and his adventurous character and unique position allowed him to enjoy deep relations with both commoners and the leaders of Indonesia. He lived his remaining 40 years in Indonesia, a country he grew to regard as his second fatherland, and his pioneering life story became the centerpiece for MBC-Television documentary *'Korean of the World'* in 2003. In his later years, he labored on 'Young Men, Go to the World With Great Ambition', a book that he hoped would be an inspiration for future generation. At present, my elder brother Shin Kee-yup continues my father's legacy as the fourth Chairman of Koreans' Association in Indonesia.

Having inherited pioneering spirit of my family, I entered Hyundai Engineering & Construction Company and decided to work for the corporation in Saudi Arabia in my late twenties. I endured harsh conditions there for two years, bleeding through the nose every morning due to extraordinarily dry climate and suffering through the violent sandstorms that swept over the country as often as once a week. Engulfed by enormous clouds of sand and dust, I often lost my way in the middle of Arabian desert. In my early thirties, I worked as a project coordinator at the construction site of Dumai Oil Refinery Factory in Sumatra, Indonesia. The experiences I gained while working in various Islamic countries during my younger days were rewarding, yet

폭넓은 교유交遊를 하며 제2의 조국 인도네시아에서 평생 개척자적 삶을 사신 선친은, 2003년 MBC-TV에서 '세계 속의 한국인'으로 선정, 방영됨으로써 널리 알려졌다.

만년에《젊은이여 세계로 웅비하라》는 후대에 귀감이 될 역저를 남기셨다. 현재 형님신기엽(辛基燁)은 인도네시아에서 4대 한인회장으로 선친의 유지를 이어가고 있다.

이런 가문의 피를 물려받은 나는 현대건설에 몸을 담아 20대 후반 사우디아라비아에서 근무하게 되었다. 건조한 날씨로 사흘 내리 아침마다 코피를 쏟고 일주일이 멀다하고 찾아드는 지독한 모래바람에 시달리는 혹독한 환경 속에서 2년을 보냈다. 때로는 아라비아사막 한가운데서 거대한 모래폭풍에 갇혀 길을 잃기도 했다.

30대 초반에는 인도네시아 수마트라 두마이정유공장 건설 현장에서 프로젝트 코디네이터로 일했다. 이러한 젊은 시절 이슬람국가에서의 체험을 남다른 보람으로 느낀 나는 연어가 회귀하듯 다시 아라비아반도로 건너와 오만, 바레인을 거쳐 현재 UAE 아부다비와 카타르를 근거지로 도화엔지니어링 GCC국가 프로젝트 수주영업 책임자로 활동하고 있다.

시단 입문은 인도네시아 두마이정유공장 공사현장을 방문한 목월선생님의 아들 박동규교수를 만난 인연에서 비롯되었다. 목월선생님은 경기중고등학교 시절 내 작품을 학원문학상, 연세대 전국백일장 장원문공부장관상으로 뽑아준 인연이 있어

like a salmon who returns to its place of birth, I returned to the Arabian Peninsula in the mid of 2000. After several years in Oman and Bahrain, I am now based in Abu Dhabi in the UAE and Doha in Qatar as a senior project development member for Dohwa Engineering Company. My main business activities entail searching for new infrastructure engineering projects in GCC countries as well as in Iraq and Jordan.

I found my opportunity to debut as a poet when Professor Dong-kyu Park, the eldest son of Poet Park Mok-wol, visited the construction site of Dumai Oil Refinery Factory.
I became acquainted with Poet Park Mok-wol while attending Kyunggi High School when he selected my literary works for Hakwon Monthly Magazine Literary Prize and Culture and Information Minister's Prize at National Writing Contest hosted by Yonsei University. Therefore, the opportunity to meet Poet Mok-wol's son after his passing in Indonesian jungle meant more to me than a mere chance encounter.

In late 1980s, I returned to Korea after being overseas in Saudi Arabia and Indonesia and found our nation struggling against military regime. As ordinary civilians organized themselves politically to pursue justice in those turbulent days, I declined comfortable corporate career I had been guaranteed for my lifetime and voluntarily joined the June 10th Uprising for Democratization in 1987, and fully devoted myself to democratization in National Assembly as Policy member and cessation of military rule. During the subsequent ten years, everyday brought new hardship and frustration alongside re-

목월선생님이 돌아가신 후 아들 박동규교수와 인도네시아 정글 현장에서의 만남은 우연 이상의 의미로 다가왔다.

사우디, 인도네시아에서 해외생활을 마치고 귀국한 1980년대 후반, 조국은 민주화의 진통을 겪고 있었다. 난세일 때 의병이 일어나듯 나는 보장받은 직장생활을 마다하고 1987년 6.10 항쟁 민주화운동에 동참해 군사정권 종식과 국회에서 법제도 민주화에 헌신했다. 이후 십년 가까운 세월은 도전과 좌절 그리고 새로운 희망을 꿈꾸는 모색과 극복의 나날이었다.
한국을 소재로 한 상당수 시편들은 80년대 후반, 90년대 초반의 정치적 상황이 만들어낸 어려운 한 시대를 정면으로 부딪쳐 온 한 지식인의 왜곡된 정신적 질서를 회복하고자 하는 순례의 과정이자 흔적이다.

시는 부조리한 세상을 향해 던지는 날카로운 칼이 될 수도 있다. 또한 접히고 구겨진 우리 인간 본래의 심성을 펴주고 위무해 주는 따뜻한 손길이 될 수도 있다.
나는 이 시대의 시는 이 양자를 다 취할 수 있어야 그 기능을 회복하고 존재가치를 인정받을 수 있다고 본다. 이런 의미에서 시란 다른 문학이나 사회, 자연과학 영역과 마찬가지로 정직한 현실 속에 뿌리내리고 그 자양을 통해 스스로 단련하면서 자생력을 길러야 한다.
이 영한시집을 내게 된 동기는 한국이 세계 10위권 경제 위상에도 불구하고 한국어를 읽을 수 있는 세계인이 0.8%에 불과

newed dreams and hope for the future. Quite a few poems that I have written about my country are the result of confronting Korea's political situation in late 1980s and early 1990s. These works would be the trace of pilgrimage made by one intellectual hoping to return to normalcy amidst an atmosphere of strife and social discord.

Poetry can be a sharp knife thrown at an absurd world. It can also be a tender hand that unfolds and pacifies our human self when it has been crumpled and abused. In our age, I believe that poetry can be of service and value only when it performs the role of both, a sharp knife and a tender hand. This notion applies to other fields of literature as well as social and natural sciences. All should be rooted in an honest reality and, in receiving nourishment from its roots, challenge themselves to be self-sufficient.

I was motivated to publish this poetry book when I learned that, although Republic of Korea enjoys honor of being 10th largest economy in the world, only 0.8 percent of world's population is able to read Korean. While living among diverse people such as Indonesians and Arab people, moreover, I realized my desire to convey my impression of their culture and the sorrow and joy that I had experienced with them.

The foundation upon which our world is based, is the human self and the natural order to which we belonged to. Despite brilliant advance in technology, however, I feel that human nature is deteriorating while nature is losing its true identity.

하다는 충격적인 통계를 접하고서였다.

나는 아랍인, 인도네시아인 등 세계인들과 생활하며 그들과 함께 겪은 삶의 애환과 생각을 공유하며 나누고 싶었다.

이 세상의 근본은 인간이며, 인간이 속한 자연인데, 첨단과학의 발달에도 불구하고 인간성은 갈수록 황폐해져 가고 자연은 본연의 모습을 잃어가고 있다. 21세기 새로운 협력과 화합으로 나아가야할 우리 인간세계는 어리석게도 근시안적 종파와 배타적 이익의 틀에서 벗어나지 못하고 지구촌 곳곳에서 유례없는 갈등을 겪고 있다.

영국의 소설가이자 수필가인 서머셋 모음이 《인간의 굴레》 Of Human Bondage에서 갈파했듯이 우리는 거추장스러운 인습의 굴레, 인간관계, 정치, 종교에 이르기까지 촘촘한 그물망에 둘러싸여 갇힌 새같이 버둥거리다 참된 자유를 누리지 못하고 생을 마감하는 것은 아닐까.

세속의 바다를 헤엄치는 나는 아이러니컬하게도 적지 않은 나이에 대칭적인 그 무엇을 꿈꾸고 있다. 우리가 껴안아야 할 진정 소중한 것은 생의 본질적인 자유와 영혼까지 사색하는 인간 존재에 대한 성찰일 것이다. 내 자신도 다 알 길 없는 열정, 혼돈, 자기 모순의 굴레 속에서 또 다시 개척해 나가야 할 앞길이 어떠한 모습으로 다가올 것인지, 나는 늘 희망과 위기의 벼랑 끝에 함께 서 있음을 느낀다.

Societies of 21st century should be proceeding towards new, enlightened form of cooperation and harmony, but we foolishly seem unable to get rid ourselves of near-sighted factionalism and an obsession with profits. As a result, an unprecedented number of conflicts are erupting in every corner of our planet.

As Sommerset Maugham, English novelist and essayist, wisely asked in *Of Human Bondage*, "are we no more than birds caught in the burdensome bondages of convention, human relations, politics and religion, like a bird wriggling in a tight net, unable to truly be free?"

Ironically, as I swim through this world, I still have dreams of those who are much younger. The things we should genuinely embrace and hold as precious are our honest reflection on human existence and those thoughts that can illuminate our soul and basic freedom. As I ponder my way, I should travel my future life with still immeasurable passion, chaos, with self-contradiction. I find myself perpetually standing on the edge of a cliff where both hope and crisis co-exist.

It will be a greatest honor if this English-Korean poetry book spurs communication and mutual understanding between Koreans and foreign people. I hope this will give us a chance to contemplate the dire straits into which our world has fallen and, in whatever small way, would provide love and consolation to those who thirst to replenish their soul.

I have a few people to express my warm-hearted thanks. I am

이 영한시집이 한국인과 이슬람인 등 세계인 사이에 새로운 소통의 단초가 되어 상호 이해의 폭을 넓히는 가운데 위기에 처한 지구환경을 돌이켜 보는 계기가 되고, 영혼의 샘물이 갈급한 이들에게 작으나마 사랑과 위안이 된다면 더없는 보람이겠다.

마음으로부터 감사를 표시하고 싶은 몇 분이 있다.
저자에 대한 깊은 애정으로 시를 영역해 주신 시인이자 출판인, 전 나이지리아대사 이동진님께 큰 은혜를 입었다. 권두환 교수님과 최시한교수님은 과학적 통찰력과 분석을 통해 제 시를 새롭게 해석해 주셨다. 특별히 번영하는 한국의 문화적 관점에서 사려깊은 코멘트를 해주신 권태균 UAE대사님과 정기종 카타르대사님께 감사드린다.

그리고 저와 같이 외국인으로 중동에서 일하고 있는, 같이 일할 때나 떨어져 있을 때나 항상 인생의 동행자인 힐러리씨와 언제나 좋은 믿음직한 친구인 터키 마스터 엔지니어 가즈 다리지씨에게 존경과 감사를 드린다. 또한 정교한 마무리가 되도록 도와준 하버드 로스쿨에 갓 입학한 총명한 조카, 이준에게도 고마운 마음을 전한다.

무엇보다 중동과 동남아 해외현장에서 때로는 자신의 목숨까지 바치며 일하고 있는 수많은 한국인과 외국 근로자들의 보

greatly indebted to poet & publisher, Lee Dong-Jin, former Korean Ambassador to Nigeria, who translated my poems into English with deep affection towards me. I am also grateful to Professor Kwon, Doo-hwan & Novelist Professor Choi Si-han who provided new interpretation in my poems by analyzing my poems with inner thoughtful scientific insight. I wish to express special thanks to Korean Ambassador to UAE, Kwon, Tae-kyun & Ambassador to Qatar, Chung, Ki-jong who presented congratulatory comments from the viewpoint of flourishing Korean Culture in Middle East region. I can not miss two expatriates, my dear life time friend, Mr. Hilary Fernandes who always along with me in the Middle East even away from me & good trustful friend, Mr. Gazi Darici, Turkish master engineer acquainted in Abu Dhabi, UAE.

I also owe to my bright nephew, Lee Joon, who just entered Harvard law school for elaborate screen supporting me.

Without invisible help & encouragement by so many others including overseas construction & engineering workers encountered in Middle East & South East Asia, these poems would not be born to this world. I would like to express my sincere gratitude to their dedication sometime even to death in the project sites and thanks to God who created this world.

Finally, I would like to dedicate these poems to my father, mother in Heaven and my beloved brilliant, virtuous youngest brother, Shin Kee Wook who passed away at 7 years old but still alive, breathes in my heart.

January 2014
Shin, Kee Sup

이지 않는 도움과 격려가 없었다면 오늘의 이 시집이 세상에 태어날 수 없었을 것이다. 이 모든 분들과 이 세상을 창조하신 신께 감사드립니다.

끝으로 하늘나라에 계신 아버님, 어머님 그리고 7살 어린 나이에 이 세상을 여의었으나 언제나 내 가슴 속에 살아 숨쉬고 있는, 총명하며 덕성스러운 사랑하는 막내동생 신기욱에게 이 시집을 바칩니다.

2014년 1월
저자 신기섭

제1부 아라비아사막의 장미석

Part One *Rose Stone in Arabian Sand*

Rose Stone

- Rose Stone in Arabian Sand

How long should we wait
until we are able to be one?

Shall we remain separated from each other
like constellation in the night sky,
keeping their position, never changing?

With my whole naked body,
and breast split by 50℃ degree heat
I desperately creep towards you to be united,
but as soon as we run against each other
we scatter in different direction.

In lonesome territory we were accustomed to,
only hungry sound of wind returned,
turned into an empty echo
after running breathlessly on the surface of the desert.

How can we become one?
In this barren land that not allows us
even a streak of liquid,
how can we be united as one?

장미석

- 아라비아사막의 장미석〈Rose stone〉

얼마를 기다려야
우리는 하나가 될 수 있는가.

밤하늘 별자리마냥 제 자리 지키듯
우리는 그저 떨어져 있어야 하는가.

50℃ 땡 불더위에 갈라 터진 가슴
맨 몸으로, 전신으로
너를 향해 부대껴가나
부딪치는 그 순간,
우리는 흩어져갈 뿐

언제나 허전한 우리의 영토엔
사막의 지평 내달아온
헛헛한 바람소리만
빈 메아리 되어 되돌아왔었지.

무엇으로 우리는 하나가 될 수 있는가.
우리를 맺어준 한 가닥 점액질조차
허락 않는 척박한 이 땅에서
우리는 어떻게 하나로 결합될 수 있는가.

모래알들은 저 스스로 휩쓸려

Grains of sand are willingly swept by wind
to wander the highest heaven.
Making whirlwinds,
cutting their bones and flesh,
by escaping the reach of wild wind
they creep into the torn surface of the desert.

Without pause, obstinately,
they crush their bodies,
and bore into densified skin
that has piled.

Then, borrowing the tide strength from the moon,
the slow and steady high tide
on the last night in lunar calender
they resolutely gather
their scattered selves
by rolling over themselves for such a long time
and finally engage in a heated embrace,
reborn themselves.

With the pattern of roses
perfectly engraved on the breast,
Salt stones that grow like mushroom,
push out with their whole bodies
in splendid climax.

아득한 구천을 헤매다
회오리치며,
제 뼈와 살을 깎으며
광포한 바람의 사정거리를 벗어나
사막의 표피 헤집고 파고든다.

기존의 응집된 각질 속으로
천착한다.
쉬임없이 집요하게
제 몸을 으깨어

그리하여
저무는 그믐밤
밀려오는 파도의 둔중한 힘
달의 인력을 빌려
오오랜 뒤채임 끝
흩어진 낱낱의 제 분신
뜨겁게 포옹하며
새롭게 탄생한다.

장미의 문양
가슴에 오롯이 새기고
버섯처럼 자라나는 소금돌,
그 화려한 절정
온몸으로 밀어낸다.

Oh, stone flowers more beautiful,
more dazzling than any flagrant flowers
in this world!

---

* Remark: 'Qatar National Museum' designed in the shape of rose stone by French designer, Jean Nouvel, is being built by South Korean leading contractor, Hyundai Engineering & Construction Co., Ltd. in Doha, Qatar capital city since Oct. 2011 aiming to be completed by end of 2014.

아,

이 세상

그 어느 향기로운 꽃보다

더 아름답고 찬연한 돌꽃이여 —

---

* 프랑스 Designer Jean Nouvel이 장미석(Rose Stone) 문양으로 설계한 '카타르 국립
  박물관' 이 현대건설에 의해 2011년 10월 착공되어 2014년 말 완공을 목표로 카타르
  수도 도하에서 시공 중에 있다.

One Day in Arabian Sand

Pestered by the wind,
it flowed off endlessly.

As the countless numbers
of sparkling, shining eyes became, at times
a large looking glass of dazzling brightness,
the grains of sand, driven from top
to bottom by the wind coming over dune,
flowed uniformly like water.

The gentle dune, touching the sky,
seemed to have held their place
without change for tens of thousands of years.
On occasion, a procession of caravan arrived
with camels and a long tail that disappeared
on a corner of dune's bosom,
Yet it was merely a silhouette being thrown
on our world.

Nothing but empty space, remains as it is.

Under suffocating, broiling heat of the sun,
everyone was laid bare, their whole bodies
unable to find cover,

어느 날의 아라비아사막

그저 바람 따라 부대끼며
끝없이 흘러내리고 있었다.

반짝이는 억만의 초롱한 눈망울
때로는 눈부신 거대한 채경이 되어
모래알 입자는 위로부터 아래로
구릉을 넘어서는 바람의 갈기에 채여
물처럼 균일하게 흐르고 또 흘렀다.

완만한 구릉은 하늘과 맞닿아
천년만년 늘상 그 자리에 그대로 있는 듯싶었다.
더러 캐러밴 행렬이 낙타무리를 이끌고
가슴 한 켠에 얹혀 긴 꼬리를 사렸지만
그건 이승의 그림자놀이에 불과했다.

늘상 빈 공간이 전부였다.

숨 막히는 불볕
숨지 못하는 전신 송두리째 드러내 놓고
다함께 뜨겁게 달아올랐다가
밤이면 서늘한 별빛과 달빛 속에
주검처럼 고요히 묻혔다.

사막은 아무 것도 없음으로 하여

becoming red hot together,
and at night, were buried peacefully like corpses
in the cool light of stars and moon.

Because nothing existed in the desert,
it was infinitely clean and beautiful.
Its landscape was more moving
than any other in the world.

In the desert from time to time,
a hoarse voice blew past
sounding like an empty wind...
That was all, nothing else.

One night, the Scorpion in night sky
Descended, bit my ankle,
And ascended again.

I left the desert lonely after I buried
my soul, which had been worn to rag.

그지없이 깨끗하고 아름다웠다.
이 세상 그 어느 풍경보다 감동적이었다.

사막엔 이따금
허허한 바람 같은 쉰 목소리가 스쳐갔다.
그 뿐이었다.

어느 날 밤하늘에 걸렸던
전갈의 별자리가 내려와 내 발목을 물고는 다시금
하늘로 올라갔다.

그 사막에 나는 누더기가 된 내 영혼을 묻어놓고
떠나왔다.

Song of Desert -1

The immense bosom of yours
where, embracing a handful of longing,
suddenly sink
like a shooting star
falling onto.

Tempered by scorching sun
the embers join together
rolling in the pattern of waves,
flowing seeming to stop,
stop seeming to flow
endless heredity.

The anxiety of existence
keeping us awake
though close eyes...

The night sky where crescent moon
hanging at an angle,
the scorpion constellation
quickly moves itself
to the top of the sky in fear
and fixes its eyes on me.

사막의 노래 -1

변방으로 지는 유성처럼
문득
한 줄기 그리움 안고
함몰하는
그대 크나큰 품속.

한나절 불볕 시련에 담금질한
불씨들은 한데 어우러져
물결무늬 일렁이며
멈춘 듯 흐르다가
흐르는 듯 멈춰서는
끝없는 유전.

눈을 감아도
잠들 수 없는 실존의 불안.

초승달 비껴 걸린 밤하늘엔
어느 결엔가 성큼
하늘 정수리로 걸음 옮겨
나를 노리는 전갈의 별자리.

10년 전
사막에 묻어둔
젊은 내 목숨의 불씨,

The embers of my youth
I buried in the desert
ten years ago,

Turned to the whistling
reviving so pure, young sound in those days
from Arabian Peninsula, crossing Yellow River,
bursts forth on a street in Seoul.

아라비아반도에서 황하를 건너뛰어
오늘 황사의 서울거리에서
북받쳐 일어서는
푸르디 푸른
휘파람소리.

Song of Desert -2

- To the *Bedouins Who Lost Their Hometown

The footprints of camels
treading, as if circling a corridor,
the edge of a burning desert.

The heartless hill
by raising whirlwinds,
sweep down to sand ash,
yesterday's horizon disappeared
without any trace,

Even sand dunes
where one can pause for breath,
kicked by the wind's high manes,
are hurled to the limitless bosom of the desert,
and gone forever.

The land of patience
where the bottom cannot be touched,
A place to stay is rejected,
This cursed land,
Even God turned away.
But you cultivate honestly
Your livelihoods,
while thankful to God instead.

---

* Bedouin: a member of a nomadic tribe of Arabs

사막의 노래 -2

- 고향 잃은 *베드윈족에게

회랑을 돌듯
열사의 끝을 디디며
떨구고 간 낙타발자국.

회오리치며
흔적조차 없이
어제의 지평선
사진沙塵으로 쓸어내리는
비정의 언덕

숨돌릴 사구砂丘조차
바람의 높은 갈기에 채여
무변無邊한 적막의 가슴에 내던져져
함몰해 버리고

더 이상
끝닿을 곳도
머무를 곳도 거부한
인종忍從의 땅,
신조차 외면한 저주詛呪의 땅,
그래도 너희들은
오히려 신에 감사하며
묵묵히 삶의 영토를 가꾸어 왔다.

---

* 베드윈 : 아라비아사막의 유목민 부족. 지금도 문명의 세계를 거부하고 사막에서 살고 있다.

Song of Desert - 3

No more drinking water could be found,
not even the promise of a fountain.
The shadow of a camel,
cast on the ground under the scorching sun,
grew smaller, turning into a spot
as black as a corpse.
Taking aim at barren head with no headwear,
the sun kindled a fire in the cracked, ruptured throat.

Before the long procession toward death
could reach the end of day,
the disorderly, wild dance of a flock of eagles,
fluttering their black veils, followed caravan.

Steep sand dunes that,
wet in the angled moonlight, climbed
as if crossing the threshold of life and death.
Sand castles collapsed
as if sinking into a pit.

The man who ventured ahead found a spring at last.
Water was as clear as the color of their transparent life.
Camels rushing ahead, hurried to quench their thirst,
Besides Camels, the man once again waited patiently.

사막의 노래-3

물은 떨어지고 샘은 기약조차 없었다.
불볕아래 드리운 낙타 그림자
주검처럼 까맣게 조여들고
*고뜨라 벗긴 정수리 겨냥한 해는
갈라터진 목줄에 불을 당겼다.

죽음을 향한 긴 행렬이 하루해를 넘기기도 전에
검은 너울 너풀거리며 뒤따르는 독수리 떼의 어지러운 난무,

생사의 문턱을 넘나들듯
비낀 달빛 적시며 오르는 가파른 사구砂丘
허방다리 짚듯 무너져 내리는 모래성.

앞서간 사내가 샘을 마침내 찾아냈다.
투명한 삶의 빛깔처럼 샘은 맑았다.
낙타가 저 먼저 서둘러 목을 축이는 곁에서
또다시 사내의 기다림은 시작되었다.
샘을 찾아 헤맬 때의 갈증보다
더한 고통과 유혹이
타는 목젖을 윽죄어 왔으나
하나, 둘 〈그들〉이 된 그는 기다리고 또 기다렸다.
마지막 일행이 와 닿았을 때는
한나절이 하얗게 바랜 어스름 녘이었다.

Pain and temptation, worse than the thirst
suffered while wandering to find the spring,
choked his burning throat, but as one of them
he waited and waited until
each arrived one after the other.
When the last arrived, it was already dusk,
the day nearly passing into the night.

With the twilight on their backs,
they drank all together.
Stirring the sky with its outstretched neck,
the camel belched to show
its thirst had been quenched.

As a streak of wind rose suddenly,
the broad leaves of palm tree
shining against the golden backlight,
placed on each of their foreheads
as if a wreath of grace
down from heaven.

황혼을 등에 이고
그들은 다 같이 물을 마셨다.
낙타가 길게 목을 빼 하늘을 휘저으며
해갈의 트림질을 걸러내고
문득 이는 한 줄기 바람결에
황금빛 역광逆光받아 번쩍이는 야자수 넓은 잎사귀,
강림하듯 그들의 이마위에 은총의 화환을 씌워 주었다.

---

* 고뜨라 : 아랍인들의 전통적인 두건

Song of Desert - 4

They fought to death
against intruders from strange civilization
who had defiled their forefathers land.
Their life-or-death struggle, tangled
with whirlwinds of yellow sand,
continued for months and years.

Drops of fresh blood
scattered everywhere
on desolate desert....

Oh, do not look back!
Following your footprints
driven from your homeland,
dense clouds of sand shuddered and rose.
The crying of sand grains
covered the sun, erased the moon,
and, swept even your silhouettes
that grew dimmer in the distance,
you who were chased
by starlight coming from afar,
were forced to sleep on dunes
without a guiding post.

사막의 노래 - 4

아버지의 영토를 더럽히는
낯선 문명의 틈입자와 오간
사막의 사투死鬪는
황사의 회오리에 뒤엉켜
해와 달을 넘겼다.

황폐한 사막 곳곳에 흩뿌려진 선혈鮮血...

돌아보지 마라,
쫓겨 가는 너희들 발자취 따라
몸서리치며 일어나는
자욱한 모래알 울음소리
해를 덮고 달을 지우며
먼 별빛에 쫓기는 너희들
희미하게 멀어져가는 실루엣마저 쓸어 덮어
지표指標없는 사구에 잠재우고

사진沙塵이 채 가시지 않은
순결한 젖가슴 파헤치며
깊숙이 꽂히는 납빛 독아毒牙,
검은 피를 뽑아 올리며
치솟는 불기둥 아래 환호하는 무리들...

배고픔과 목마름의 사선死線을 넘어

Leaden fangs, digging into
the chaste bosom where a dust-storm lingers,
driven deeply into the earth.
Crowds that, extracting black blood,
shouted with joy under a soaring pillar of fire....

Crossing the line between life and death, hunger and thirst,
your forefathers land was defended
but now you feel great sorrow
that it can be yours no more.
In sunny tombs where all were buried together
sleep saw-toothed sand mounds
carrying stones on their heads.

With fear your enemies might know
the sound of crying camels
breaking the silence
of deep night in the desert.

Turning over in bed to face Mecca
amidst thick fragrance of jasmine
that circles the plateau,
your soul, soaked in cold moonlight,
breathes through shining, white bones.

지켜왔던 아버지의 영토
더 이상 저희 건이 될 수 없는 크나큰 슬픔,
함께 묻힌 해받이 무덤엔
톱날 선 모래문이 돌을 이고 잠들어
적이 알까 두려운 낙타 울음소리
적막을 깨치는 사막의 깊은 밤

고원을 휘도는 자스민 그윽한 향기 속에
메카 향해 돌아누운 당신의 넋은
하얗게 빛나는 뼈마디로
차가운 달빛에 젖어 숨 쉬고 있다.

Song of Desert - 5

- While Crossing Arabian Desert

On the day I left for my new post
with my belongings packed,
the sandy storm followed
and wept for me.

Like our ancestors who left their homes
for Manchu, we, young men, leave
for a barren, far away land
where the Arabian princess that we dreamt of
no longer exists.
No room, not even the romance
to sing for all humble ones,
as seaman's farewell song.

A sandstorm blocked the desert road,
a solitary lifeline to grope for,
and erased the sky, earth, horizon,
everything on ground,
rocked the wholeness from sky to earth.

High-beamed headlight was helpless
in the maze, visible by not even an inch.
Riding on a whirlwind,
sand dunes rose suddenly.

사막의 노래 - 5

- 사막을 건너며

짐보따리 챙겨
임지任地로 떠나던 날,
모래바람이 따라와
함께 울어 주었다.

꿈속에 그리던 아라비아공주는
더 이상 존재하지 않는
척박한 이역의 땅,
우리네 조상들이
북간도北間道를 찾아 떠나듯
젊은 우리들은 떠나간다.
흔하디흔한 뱃가락 이별가를 뽑는
한 가닥 낭만도 없이.

외줄기 목숨처럼
더듬어가던 사막의 길 차단하며
하늘, 땅, 지평선
지상의 모든 것
일체를 지우며
온 천지를 일렁이는 모랫바람.

하이빔 켠 헤드라이트 불빛도
속수무책일 뿐
한 치 앞 가늠할 수 없는 미로迷路

Then, the wind scattered in the air
fine grains like soft hail
while violently churning
vast and boundless space,
swept the hills of the desert,
to be strewn at the end of the sky.

The countless rebellion of sand grains,
once dead, but, warmed hot by silence,
revive and rise up individually
to proclaim to the world their existence
Now the desert, at last, becomes worthy of its name
and all living things once moving
become silent under its presence.

The chaos, magnificent spectacle of Creation.
Sand grains, blowing away in the boundless sky,
feel uneasy in anticipation of the new order
that they are soon to meet.

Will a new day come to this world?
when the sand storm stops, as if it never came,
after the grains fully covered car windows running desert,
finally erased the eyes, noses, mouths
of those who are alive,
our dirty selfishness,
and, having filled our windpipes,
discard the very trace of us as sand mummies, in the

모래둔덕은 돌개바람타고 치솟아 올라
싸락눈 같은 미립자를 공중분해 시켜
드넓은 아라비아사막
막막한 공간 왼통 휘저어
사막의 구릉 모조리 휩쓸어
하늘 끝으로 날려 버린다.

죽었던 존재,
침묵으로 뜨겁게 달군
살아있는 낱낱이
스스로를 알리는
헤아릴 수 없는
무수한 모래알들의 반란.
사막은 비로소 사막다워지고
살아 움직이던 일체의 모든 것
그 앞에서 침묵한다.

천지창조의 혼돈과 장관
가없는 허공에 휘날리는 모래알들은
맞이할 새로운 질서의 예감으로 설렌다.

차창을 뒤덮은 모래알 입자가
살아있는 우리들의 눈과 코와 입을 지우고
추잡한 이기의 욕망을 지우고
우리들의 숨구멍마저 저들로 채워
사막 가운데 모래 미이라로 흔적을 버린 후
언젠가 거짓말인 듯
모래바람이 잦아들 때 이 세상에도 새 날이 올까.

desert?

Will the new day come, when
all existing horizons are reversed
the highs and lows on earth
take their positions in new order?

Oh, this great revolution by the desert,
which may happen
at any time, perhaps now!

모든 질서의 지평선 뒤바꾸고
지상의 높고 낮음
새로운 질서 속에 자리 잡는
그런 새로운 날,
펼쳐질 수 있을까.

아아,
지금도 무시로 일어나고 있을
사막의
이 위대한 혁명.

To a Palestinian Friend I Met
in Saudi Arabia

Wandering at the end of 20th century
without having a passport.

Without even a square inch of land
in this earth for your own,
it is a sin that you married.

Cherishing memory of you
and your family to whom I said goodbye
eight years ago, I was drunk yesterday
on makgeolli,* rice wine,
with Korean-style sausage in mutton's stead.

When I woke up from hangover,
my stomach groaned out of discomfort.

Amel, are you still roaming,
like an animal, with your family
in a tent overlooking Red Sea?
Do you continue to wander about
from place to place with no destination,
treading on starlights in the desert
like a wild, stray dog?

사우디아라비아에서 만난
팔레스타인 친구에게

패스포트도 없이
떠도는 20세기말의 방황.

지구상 어느 곳,
땅 한 평 없는 네가 결혼한 것은
죄악이다.

8년 전 헤어진 너와 네 일가붙이를 생각하면서
어제 양고기 대신 순대 곁들인
*막걸리를 취하도록 마셨다.

숙취에서 깨어나니 뱃속이 거북살스레
꾸루룩거리더구나.

아멜, 너는 시방도
홍해바다 굽어보이는 텐트에서
짐승처럼 가족들과 섞여 뒹굴면서
집 없는 그곳 들개처럼 사막의 별빛을
밟고 정처 없이 떠다니느냐.

위, 창자 어디에도 동화되지 못하고
밤새 내 뱃속에서 떠도는 막걸리처럼...
아니면
광포한 모래바람에 스스로를 찢어

Like makgeolli wandering my insides
all through the night, absorbed
neither in my stomach nor intestines…

Oh, Amel, my friend!
did you shred yourself
to blow away with the violent, sandy wind?

---

* makgeolli : Korean traditional rice wine

날려 보냈는가.

아멜, 나의 친구여.

---

* 막걸리 : 쌀로 빚어 만든 한국 전통술

Deep Sleep of an Offshore Worker

- In memory of the industrial warrior of Hyundai Engineering &
Construction Co. who confronted death when attacked by Iraqi
Missile while working for the Oil Gas Separation Unit on *Marzan
offshore, Saudi Arabia

So clean and pure Arabian Sea
where the clearest and most transparent light,
filtered from the sky,
joins with brilliant waters.

The Sea of Peace
Still dampening my pillow,
always rolling like the sea
in my home town, wets me, calms me,
by opening crossbar in the boundless heart.

Mixture of sea's various blues,
melting into my heart, were more
splendid and elegant than rainbow colors.
Even the furious whirlwind of desert
held its breath meekly around your feet.

Around that time, dolphins appeared,
occasionally along ship route
alternating between lead and follower.
They ran through bobbing wave,
some jumping to top of the mast,

수부의 깊은 잠

- 사우디아라비아 마르잔 해상가스분리공사* 중 이락의 미사일
  공격으로 산화한 현대건설 산업 전사를 추모하며

하늘빛 중
가장 맑고 투명한 빛살 걸러내
현란한 물이랑 함께 어우러진
순결무구한 아라비아바다

시방도
베갯잇 적시며 고향바다처럼
늘 출렁이며 나를 적시며 달래며
드넓은 마음의 빗장 열어주는
화평의 바다.

가슴에 풀어놓은 푸른 색상의 배합은
무지개빛보다 화려하고 단아했었고
광포한 사막의 회오리도
네 발치에선 저근덧 숨을 죽였었다.

그 무렵 돌고래떼 무리지어
가끔씩 뱃길 따라 나타나
앞서거니 뒤서거니
어깨춤 들썩이는 파도이랑 짓치며
더러는 마스트 끝으로 튀어 올라

presented a variation to a monotonous voyage.

It was really unexpected comfort to the seafaring men,
armed with copper brown muscles who marked their lives
upon a buoy, always rolling.

At Banguhjin* inlet off, Ulsan City
offshore worker looked away deliberately
from his hometown hill growing smaller and smaller.
Tugging an iron barge as immense as mountain,
He passed South China Sea, Sri Lanka as well.
The whipping of rainstorm was nothing to him,
letting the wind, that was
cooling his bead of sweat,
lightly wiped it off.

What can be harder than the agonies
he had suffered in the past?
The paralyzing nightmare on concrete forest,
the wretched days spent crushing
barren soil with an empty heart,
today he escaped to opulent sea.
The hope in his palpitating hearts fluttered
as vigorously as the flag on the mast
and his desires rose
as high as the extended height of barge crane
soaring upon the ship.

단조로운 항해 끝의 변조變調를 선사하며
늘상 출렁이는 부표浮漂 위에
삶의 푯대를 세워야 하는
구릿빛 근육질 사내들에게
뜻밖의 위안을 안겨주기도 했었지.

울산 앞바다 방어진포구
멀어져가는 고향 언덕 짐짓 눈썹 끝에 지우고
산같이 거대한 철구조물 바지선을 이끌고
남지나해 건너 스리랑카 가로질러
까짓 거
몰아치는 폭풍우의 시련쯤이야
쓰윽
한 줄기 땀방울 식히는
바람결에 씻어내면 그만이었다.

아무려면 지난날의 고뇌만 하랴.
콘크리트 숲에 가위 눌리던 악몽,
황량한 박토薄土 빈 가슴으로 으깨야 했던
참담한 날들 청산하고
풍요의 바다로 탈출해 온 오늘,
설레는 바람은 마스트 깃발같이
힘차게 나부끼고
소망의 끝은 바벨탑같이 굳건히 치솟은
해상 바지선 크레인의 돋운 키만큼이나
까마득히 높았었다.

Diving to the heart of sea
where transparent light gestures merrily,
he washed off old, earthly dirt
and saw fishes' group dancing,
naturally splendid color and shape
that drew close to his widened chest.
His poverty on the ground, recompensed
fully more or less.

Lying on rolling deck with his body warmed
by scorching heat of the day,
he began to doze
listening to monotonous sound of the engine
like a lullaby.
Stillness pervaded everything,
even the sounds of waves were heard no more.
On the construction site of Mazran Maritime Terminal,
rushing breathlessly towards completion,
everyone fell into a siesta.

Then, the daily order was upheaved
by thundering sound
with glittering flashes.

The body of the ship, sunk
by sudden bombardment.

The angry waves of Arabian Sea soared high.

투명한 햇살 해살거리며 손짓하는
해심海心을 향해 자맥질하면
지산의 묵은 때 말끔히 행구고
제 본래의 황홀한 빛과 자태로
가슴 한 가득 안겨오는 물고기떼의 군무群舞
지상에서의 빈곤,
넉넉히 보상되고도 남았다.

한 나절 불볕아래 달궈진 육신
흔들리는 갑판에 누워
단조로운 엔진을 자장가 삼아
설핏 선잠에 빠져들 때
문득 파도소리마저 끊긴 듯
파고드는 적막,
피크peak를 향한 숨 가쁜
마즈란 해상터미널 공사 현장
한식경의 오수에 잠길 즈음

일상의 질서
송두리째 뒤집는 굉음과 번쩍이는 섬광
느닷없는 포격에 함몰하는 작업선 동체,
치솟는 아라비아바다의 성난 물결
튕겨 오르는 사내의 팔다리
파편 따라 널브러진 해면海面

찰라 엔 듯 스쳐 간 울산 고향 앞바다
눈 속에 꼬옥 담고

The leg and arm of offshore worker,
bouncing up in the air,
scattered on the sea alongside splinters.

Holding tightly in his eye the open sea of Ulsan,
his hometown, flashing by him,
the man submerged into deep sea.

The broken mast, torn flag,
along with his miserably frustrated desire
floated, side by side, over the wave
in this world, full of sin.

---

* Remark: Marzan offshore construction period: Aug 1982 - April 1986
* Banguhjin: eastern part of Ulsan Port(known as Hyundai city) located South
  Eastern Korean peninsular, famous for frequent appearance of Whales

바다 속으로 잠수하는 사내

부러진 마스트 찢긴 깃발,
무참히 꺾인 사내의 소망
나란히 죄 많은 이승의 물이랑을 넘고 있다.

---

* 마즈란 해상기지 공사 기간 : 1982.8. ~ 1986.4.
* 방어진 : 현대시로 알려진 한반도 동남에 위치한 울산 동쪽지역으로 고래가 자주 출몰한다.

Dark Evening Over Red Sea

- Looking Back on a Day in 1979

Worthy descendants of the Phoenicians,
those who once swept over the Mediterranean,
Lebanese people,
Have dropped anchor at every beautiful Middle Eastern
harbor,
Are proud of their elegant manners,
Their adroit business acumen.

Foreigners, enjoying the cool sea breeze,
take mutton, well-roasted like the glow of the setting
sun,
hanging at the end of the spire of Lebanese restaurant
resembling the Al-hambra Palace.
They lift glasses of non-alcoholic beer
with dates thicker than honey, their snack.

The descendants of the Bedouin are so familiar
with the pasture that they sleep outdoors
under the starlight of the desert.
Their new apartments,
built for them by the Saudi government,
house the sheep they raise.

Somewhere between their tents, Amel,

홍해 어두운 저녁녘

- 1979년 어느 날 회상

일찍이 지중해를 석권했던
페니키아인의 후예답게
레바논인들은
중동 아름다운 항구마다 닻을 내리고
세련된 매너, 능란한 상술을 뽐내고 있다.

알함브라궁을 닮은 레바논인 레스토랑 첨탑 끝에
걸린 붉은 낙조마냥
잘 익은 양고기, 함께 곁들인 알코올 없는 맥주잔
꿀보다 진한 대추야자를 간식 삼아
이방인들은 시원한 바닷바람을 즐긴다.

사우디정부가 지어준 최신식 아파트에
기르던 양들을 대신 들여보내고
아직도 사막의 별빛 아래 노숙露宿하는 게 편한,
방목放牧에 익숙한 베드윈 자손들.

그네들의 텐트 틈새 어디쯤엔가
새끼고양이만 같은 바글바글한 아이들
시커먼 맨발에 광대뼈 드러낸 아낙을 거느린
나의 팔레스타인 친구, 아멜이 함께 뒹굴고 있다.

짙푸른 물결 일렁이는 홍해바다
수평선은 이미 어둠의 장막에 가려

my Palestinian friend, who has a wife with black bare feet
and protruded cheekbones, is rolling on the floor
with swarming children as small as kitten.

The Red Sea, where dark blue waves swell.
The horizon, already hidden by the curtains of darkness,
has collapsed into the night sky.
How far away from your hometown,
no one can promise to return back.

The deeper the night,
the blackened eyes of poor children
shine brighter with curiosity.

Amel, my friend, who gave me, instead of bread,
a mournful song of wandering
that flowed from the strings of guitar.
At that time, untamed wild dogs,
pacing around restlessly,
snarling fiercely.

One anxious day in the life of a stateless man,
trying to survive the uneasiness
that creeps stealthily into his heart.
I wonder why this tiresome day has been revived
so freshly in my memory....

밤하늘로 함몰해 버리고
기약조차 할 수 없는 너의 고향길은
또 얼마나 아득한 것인지...

밤이 깊을수록
가난한 아이들 까만 눈망울은
더욱 호기심으로 환히 불을 켜고

빵 대신 기타줄로 애조 띤 방랑의 노래를 선사하는
나의 친구 아멜,
그 때 너의 주변을 서성이던 거친 야생野生의
들개떼의 으르릉거림.

슬며시 불안이 스멀스멀 일어나는 무국적자의 고단한 하루가
오늘 따라 왜 그리 선명하게 되살아오는 것인지...

Istanbul

Blue Mosque, with six pillars supporting the sky
on a low hill where traces of an ancient capital,
two thousand years old, remain.

Circle dance of a flock of birds,
white birds that arrive one after another
in succession as if keeping an appointment
in late evening, flying over the minaret of Mosque,
like mediums connecting this world and the one beyond.
Dolmabahche, showing Sultan's glory
of Osman Turkey, the Palace of Topkaf,
the wall of ruin, shaded houses in forest
on which the lights of twinkling stars rain down,
yachts, working boats and pleasure boats
coming and going,
Bosphorus Strait makes its grand appearance as if
altogether swept
onto a wide screen.

Travellers say a month quickly passes
for he who schedules a one week journey,
and the one who plans a month,
stays three months or 365 days, a year.
Once absorbed by Istanbul, they say,
he longs to stay there without end,
for there are more things worthy to see

이스탄불

2000년 고도古都 흔적 머무는 나지막한 구릉 위
여섯 기둥 하늘 떠받친 블루모스크.

늦은 저녁 약속이나 한 듯 하나 둘 셋... 연이어 등장해
모스크 첨탑 떠도는 저 하얀 새떼들의 원무圓舞,
저승과 이승 잇는 영매靈媒 같다.

오스만터키 술탄 영화 드러내는 돌마바흐체, 토프카프궁전,
폐허의 성곽, 숲 그늘 별빛 반짝이는 가옥들,
분주히 오가는 요트, 작업선, 유람선
대형스크린에 죄다 쓸어 담은 듯
넉넉한 품새 펼쳐 보이는 보스포러스 해협.

일주일 머물러 왔다 한 달 홀쩍 가고
한 달 머물려다 석달, 일년 삼백육십오일 넘기게 된다는,
한번 빠려들면 한없이 머물고 싶어지는,
세상 어느 곳보다 볼 것 많고 자유롭고 아기자기 재미있다는,
이슬람나라지만 생기발랄 청춘이 대낮에도 서로를 껴안는,
백년 된 Tram전차가 삐이- 경적 울리며 가로질러 가면
자신의 어깨 쳐주는 연인 대하듯 눈웃음치며 비켜서지.

널찍한 대로 곧게 뻗은 시원히 트인 번화가 들어서면
항아리 물 넘치듯 밑도 끝도 없이 밀려드는 행렬,
길모퉁이 전통악기 켜는 소녀

than at any other place in this world,
Free, charming, interesting place.
An Islamic country where lively youths embrace in broad daylight,
where a hundred-year-old tramcar,
whistling a warning, cuts the path of people,
who step aside, eyes smiling, as if facing lovers
patting them on the back.
Entering a business quarter, wide open
along the broad, straight main street,
throngs of people pouring in
endlessly like water overflowing a pot,
moreover, a girl plays the traditional instrument on a street corner
intimately melts into the landscape
nearby Taxim Square.

Oh Istanbul!
The marvelous romanticism
that turns traveling strangers
into familiar landscape.
Constantinople, where the melancholy of Osman Turkey's collapse
still continues to breathe! How dear your name is!

Under Galata Bridge
with dense clutter of fishing rods,
I enjoy the peculiarities of a mackerel kebab,
Golden Horn, where ships
restlessly carry landscapes,
I entrust part of my heart to the waves,
swelling tides coming from Black Sea
headed around Asia and Europe,
Feel myself flow, flow, flow away boundlessly.

애잔한 얼굴마저 스스럼없이 풍경으로 녹아드는
탁심 광장 언저리.

낯선 여행객도 한데 어울려 낯익은 풍경으로
만들어버리는 묘한 낭만,
콘스탄티노플, 오스만터키 몰락의 멜랑콜리 함께
살아 숨쉬는
오, 다정한 그대 이름 이스탄불!

낚싯대 촘촘히 드리운 갈라타Galata브리지 아래
고등어캐밥 별미삼아 선박들이 쉼없이 풍물 실어 나르는
골든 혼Golden Horn
찰랑이는 물결에 마음 한 자락 맡기노라면
흑해에서 흘러와 아시아, 유럽 아우른 저 넘실대는
물결이랑 따라
나 또한 흘러 흘러 끝 간 데 없이 마냥 흘러가누나.

When I Returned to the Desert

If the desert no longer keep the absolute solitude
and desolateness possessing itself,
it is no longer desert.
what will take that place for our solitude and desolation?

My homeland, numerous surgically-enhanced beauties
walking wild shamelessly, is not a bit different
from Dubai, the desert city where
the building of skyscrapers,
once taken to the end of man's sight,
suddenly ceased.

In the desert, the wind may rise at any time,
but this happens only in an empty desert.
Blocked by the walls of high buildings in an artificial
city,
the sand storm wanders,
leaving ghostly traces like a whirlwind on asphalt.

The desert is no longer a desert
if it has lost its solitude and desolateness,
like fake love packed by ghost mask.

다시 사막에 와 보니

사막이 사막다움을 잃어
그만이 간직한 절대 고독과 적막을 잃는다면
무엇이 우리의 고독과 적막을 대신해 줄 것인가.

성형미인이 염치 모르고 설쳐대는 모국이나
끝 간 데 없이 마천루를 세우다가 덜커덕 멈춰버린
사막도시 두바이나 오십보백보다.

사막에는 여전히 바람이 무시로 일어나나
그것은 허허로운 사막에서일 뿐,
인공도시 높다란 빌딩 벽에 막혀버린 모래바람은
오늘도 아스팔트 위에 회오리 같은 유령의 흔적을 남기며
떠돌고 있다.

사랑이 유령 마스크에 포장되듯
고독과 적막을 잃은 사막은 더 이상 사막이 아니다.

Desert Diary

- A Walk at Dawn

My walk began at dawn seven years ago
on the seashores of Salalah, Oman
south of the Arabian Peninsula.

In the Kingdom of Bahrain, along a long walled road
from village to village,
then, I crossed a bridge in Abu Dhabi
from Al Ban Dar to Al Muneera

I met flamingoes with deep scarlet breast
and encountered a village elder guarding Immam tomb
in the shape of a small mosque in Oman,
in Bahrain, an interior decorator caring
for a beautiful garden
while raising a nephew who lost his parents to Gulf War,
and a Bangladeshi gardener who placed a cowboy hat
on my head with silent smile,
In Abu Dhabi I greet with a nod
a tall, slender, silver-haired westerner from Cyprus
and a Chinese woman who enjoys walking only
backwards.

The backdrop is no difference
alway with red sun and blue sea.

사막일기
- 새벽 산책

7년 전 아라비아반도 남쪽 오만 살랄라
바닷가에서 시작된 새벽 산책,
걸프만 바레인에서는 마을과 마을,
긴 담장길로 이어지다가
아부다비에선 다리 건너
반 다르와 무니라섬을 오가고 있다.

오만에서는 가슴에 선홍빛 진한 홍학과
조그만 모스크 무덤 지키는 촌로,
바레인에서는 걸프전으로 부모 잃은 조카 키우며
예쁜 정원 가꾸는 실내장식업자,
말없는 미소로 카우보이모자를 머리에 얹어준
방글라데시 정원사와 해후했고
아부다비에선 키가 껑충한 은발의 사이프러스 서양인,
뒤로만 걷는 중국여자와 눈인사 나눈다.

배경은 떠오르는 붉은 해와 푸른 바다.
막간에 까만 지느러미 수면 가르며 요동치는 물고기,
바위로 기어 나와 해바라기하는 게떼,
가끔 성가신 개들도 등장한다.

간간이 지구 반대편에서
"아직도 거기 계세요?"
"언제 돌아 오냐?" 문자 오기도 한다.

Fishes rush around wildly, parting the surface
with their black fins, crabs creep on rocks for a sunbath,
sometimes bothersome dogs appear.

Now and then, messages come from the opposing side
of the earth:
"Are you still there?", "When will you come back?"
I reply: "I also wonder when I will return...
But I still have a dream to realize."

"언제 돌아가게 될지 사실 나도 궁금하오…
그러나 나는 아직 이뤄야할 꿈이 있소."

제2부 인도네시아 정글
Part Two *Indonesian Jungle*

Sunset of Tanarot

- Again in Bali

If extinction could be so magnificent,
so beautiful, I wish to die
just as I am.

This is not temptation
rather an ardent longing.

Shinbones being shaved,
an island reveals itself,
as if it were drowning in the waves
that rise high, even today, incessantly,
that spins time on a spinning wheel.
The temple, like a blooming lotus flower
on the island's stone pillar
soaring into the air dangerously.

Overcoming the
futility of an extinction
counted down our rather short living ,
women wearing Batik clothes
offer bright flowers and armful fruit
atop an erected altar.
Silver-haired tourists gather toward evening
competing on the edge of a cliff

타나롯의 일몰 日沒
- 다시 발리에서

소멸이 이토록 장엄하고
아름다울 수 있다면
지금 이대로 죽고 싶다.

이것은 유혹이 아니라
동경이다.

정강이뼈 깎으며
세월의 물레짓
오늘도 쉬임없이 짓쳐대는 파도 깃에
익사할 듯 드러나는 섬,
그 위태로운 허공의 돌기둥 위
연꽃 벙글듯 피어난 신전神殿.

늘 카운트다운에 들어가는
소멸의 허망함 딛고
쌓아올린 제단 위
오늘도 환한 들꽃과 한 움큼의 과실,
바띡 옷차림 여인들에 의해 봉양되고
해질녘에 맞춰
은발의 관광객들은 다투어
낙조와 신전이 일직선으로
가슴에 안기는 벼랑 끝으로 모여든다.
새들이 숲을 찾아 깃을 치듯...

to embrace the half destroyed temple from the leg
and glowing, setting sun in a straight line.
Like birds flapping their wings
upon finding the forest…

Did they also come here to be consoled
by the fact that death
can be so grand, so beautiful…

I see clearly red sun sinking into the sea,
the earthly, wild dance of shadows,
flickering between the temple's pillars
like a hallucination against the sun,
last moment of time, only seen vividly
upon sinking
like the fate of Caine ship.

Oh! Tanarot!
Transformed into an active volcano
burning in my heart!

그들도 죽음이
이토록 장엄하고 아름다울 수 있다는
위안을 갖기 위해 이곳을 찾아드는 것일까...

바다로 함몰하는 붉은 해
역광逆光받아 환각인양
신전 돌기둥 사이 어른거리는
이승에서의 그림자들의 난무,
케인호의 최후처럼
침몰하고야 말
시간의 끝이 뚜렷이 보인다.

오! 내 속에서 활화산으로 현신現身하여
불타는 그대, 타나롯!

Poem of Bali-1

If you arrive Bali,
time stops flowing.

The great religion
that erected towers on every house,
Mysterious dance that reproduces legend,
Festival flags of various colors
fluttering high atop bamboo sticks
are breathing, alive in their primitive state.

In the stream of nearby forest,
naked reveal themselves freely
in the bright daylight.
At dusk,
women bathe their busts
in the flowing water.
Their palpitation
hidden in their furtive gesture.

Before the curtains of the night
could draw close the silhouette of palm trees,
women are dragged away, as if plundered,
into the deep forest
at the bottom of an active volcano.

발리의 시 -1

이곳에 오면
세월의 흐름도 멈춘다.

집집마다
탑을 쌓은 위대한 종교와
전설을 재현하는 기괴한 춤
대나무 장대 높이 펄럭이는
제전祭典의 색색 깃발들이
원시 속에 살아 숨 쉬고 있을 뿐...

가까운 숲 계곡엔
벌거벗은 남성男性이 밝은 광명 속에
스스럼없이 드러나 있고
어스름 깃들 무렵이면
여인들은
흐르는 강물에 목물을 한다.
은근한 몸짓 속에 감춰진
설렘의 목물.

밤의 휘장이
야자수 실루엣을 채 걷어가기 전에
여인들은 노략질 당해 가듯
활화산 기슭 깊은 숲속으로 이끌려가고

The crying of insects, as numerous
as the stars ripening in the night sky,
join together with soaking carnal desire.

밤하늘 여무는 별만큼이나
무성한 풀벌레 울음소리
육정肉情과 어우러져 한결 흥건하다.

Poem of Bali-2

The specks of clouds that flow by slowly
with the breath of clear wind,
as if shaking off a piece of eternal time.
The orchid flowers; Angre, Kamboja
that blossom under the shadow of cloud.
Warm exchange of glance
with celestial flowers
more splendid than a rainbow.

Black soil,
from the decaying and hardening
of all things earthly
over long expanses of time,
I realized at a glance that
These are the great transformation from dirt.

발리의 시-2

해맑은 바람의 숨결 따라
천만년 세월 한 자락 떨치듯
쉬엄 흐르는 구름송이,
구름그늘 아래
벙그는 앙그레, 캄보자꽃
무지개보다 화려하게 피어나는
천상天上의 꽃과의
뜨거운 입맞춤.

그것은
긴 세월을 두고
지상의 온갖 것 다 썩고 다져져
일구어진 검은 땅,
흙의 위대한 변신變身임을
새삼 깨닫는다.

Poem of Bali - 3

Eyes suddenly opened
after a squall passed by,
snatching concentrated passion away.

Embracing the sky, sea, mountain, lake,
all these, the beauty of each
spread at its own place,
You sit calmly in the warm coolness.

The waves of South Pacific
fretful at the tip of my toes,
while the ocean spreading
limitlessly over them,
embraced all together by a sense of plenty.

Overflowing bright sunbeams everywhere,
western blondes, naked people under burning sun
wriggle their fat bodies
at Kuda seashore,
bursting sound of motorcycles
racing away in the street,
ringing like firecrackers at festival,
but Bali is always being Bali the same ever.

발리의 시-3

한 마당 격정激情 앗는
스코올 스쳐간 뒤
문득 트이는 개안開眼.

하늘, 바다, 산, 호수
두루 안아 저마다의 아름다움
제 자리에 펼쳐두고
뜨거운 서늘함 속에 웅좌雄座하고
발끝에 보채는 남태평양의 파도
그 너머 한량없이 드넓은 바다
함께 보듬는 넉넉함.

밝은 햇살은 곳곳에 넘치고
구다Kuta 해변은 금발의 벌거벗은 태양족太陽族들이
피둥한 몸뚱아리를 꿈틀대고
오토바이 폭음이 축제의 폭죽처럼 울리며 거리를 내닫지만
발리는 발리로 있을 뿐

자연 속에서
자연의 질서를 순응하는
발리인들의 순박한 품성은
흑단목각의 정교함으로
바띡의 현란한 원색무늬로 되살아나
생활을 찾고

Humble, honest character
of the Balinese, who adapt themselves
to the order of nature,
finds life through
elaborate ebony wood carving,
gorgeously patterned primary colors
of batik cloth along their life,
joined with religious celebration
Bali is always full and overflowing.

The sense of comfort,
self-sufficient abundance in their lives,

They seem poor, but never.

생활은 종교의 제전으로 한데 어우러져
늘 충만히 차고 넘친다.

자족自足함으로 하여
부여받은 삶의 여유
그 넉넉한 풍요로움.

가난하지만 결코 가난하지 않은 그들.

Poem of Bali - 4

Pure-white soul wanders
three spans of a hand
over the head of tall palm tree,
the cloud's shadow, a spot
interwoven with the dazzling sunlight,
flows on green grass field.

Old trees, entangled
as if in jungle,
carelessly shedding leaves,
one after another,
scattered on the road of our human life,
without making any sound.

Birds and animals that climb,
under the roof of a thatched house,
toward the brilliant sunlight.
Their shapes, clearly alive,
engraved as thick shadow,
tells living legend,
a dialogue of more than mere words,
as if they were tokens
left by your grandfather,
whose face you do not remember.

발리의 시-4

키다리 야자수 세 뼘 너머
떠도는 순백의 영혼,
눈부신 햇살이 직조한 구름그늘 한 점
초록의 들판위로 흘러가고

정글처럼 뒤얽힌 거대한 고목이
무심히 떨치는 한 떨기 잎새,
해거름 덮여오는 무상한 인생의 길목에
소리 없이 내려와 깔린다.

찬연한 날빛을 향해
초가지붕 밑을 기어오르는 뭇 새와 짐승,
또렷이 살아있는 형상
짙은 그늘로 음각陰刻시킨 채
얼굴을 알 수 없는 그대 할아버지가
남긴 정표인양
살아있는 전설로
말 이상의 대화를 건네며...

장대 같은 빗줄기 스쳐간
숲속의 오후,
함초롬히 피어나는 영롱한 빗물방울
두레박 퍼울려 맑은 샘물 끌어내듯
빨강, 파랑, 남빛, 주황 한데 어우러져

Afternoon time in the forest,
when heavy rain came and left.
The bright raindrops that bloom neatly.
The celestial flowers that blossom
in red, blue, indigo, yellow,
more rapturously than a rainbow,
extracted like clear water
drawn from a well using a bucket.
Each blows a bugle to its own pitch.

The sound of sea surging forth
from the tip of waves.
The last paradise on earth
where heaven and earth
join together, kissing each other.

무지개보다 황홀하게 피어나는
천상의 꽃들,
저마다의 음색音色으로 나팔을 분다.

더불어
파도 깃에 묻어나 솟구쳐 오르는
해조음海潮音
천상과 천하가 한데 얼려
입맞춤하는
이승에서의 마지막 낙원.

Three Days of Islam Funeral Ceremony

- For the Soul of the Dead

Backs leaning against the wall
on a carpet as red as blood,
for the one who left
the day before yesterday
on the forked road towards the afterworld
they pray to God, the Great for men:
"Al Hammdullila Mohammed!"
Solemn harmony for those
that, as yet remaining in this world,
encourages and strengthens one another.

Sweat emerging ceaselessly
inbetween their breasts
to be condensed into crystal drops.

Without a cup of water to quench their thirst,
they gather for their neighbor,
their fellow traveller in this life,
at a house in the forest,
overgrown with weeds,
they chant Koran endlessly,
raising their voiced together
as if strengthening the dying fire of life.

이슬람의 삼일제三日祭
- 죽은 이의 영혼을 위하여

핏빛 붉은 양탄자
벽을 등지고 앉아
엊그제 저승의 갈림길로 떠난 자를 위해
알-함두렐라 모하멧
위대한 인간의 신神
아직은 이승에 남은 자들끼리
함께 격려하며 북돋우는 장엄한 하모니.

가슴 사이 쉬임없이 돌고 또 도는
땀땀땀 땀의 농축된 결정체

마른 목 축일 물 한 잔 없이도
삶을 함께 등정하는 이웃을 위해
별꽃 무성히도 풍성한 숲속 집에 모여
언제 그칠지 모를
코란
일제히 생의 여윈 불빛 돋우듯
목청을 돋우고

한恨문은 창唱가락 같은 끈끈한 정
묻어나는 암송소리,
영혼을 가진 자에게 들려주는

The compassion as persistent as
a melody of deep regret
oozes from the sound of their recitation.
Consoling sound,
bestowed by God to those possessing soul.

On bent knees, they pray,
calling with their fingertip:
Leillalal Illoro!
Leillalal Illoro!
Leillalal Illoro!

Chorus of lament,
leading the dead soul
on the strange road to the other world.
Leillalal Illoro!
(No God except Allah!)

Their chants as if encouraging their own lives
to be called some day
to the other world.
Leillalal Illoro!
Leillalal Illoro!
Like recurring phrase of a boat song,
repeating endless.
Leillalal Illoro!
(No God except Allah!)

신의 위로소리.

무릎 꿇고 손가락 끝으로 부르는 기도
레일랄라 일롤로
레일랄라 일롤로
레일랄라 일롤로

사자死者의 낯선 저승길 인도하는
어기영차 어기영차 후렴소리
언젠가 불려갈
자신의 삶을 격려하듯
레일랄라 일롤로
레일랄라 일롤로
뱃가락 반복귀처럼
언제까지 되풀이되는
레일랄라 일롤로!
(No God except Allah!)

이 세상의 신은 오직 알라일 뿐!

가슴에서 돌아오던 땀
온 몸에 젖고 말씀에 젖어
함께 상여매고 험한 저승길 오르노라면
알아들을 길 없는 코란 말씀도
가슴을 덥힌 육성으로
적도의 열기보다 더 뜨겁게

In this world, there is no God except Allah!

The sweat from their breasts
carved on their bodies and soaking their words,
they climb the steep road to the other world,
carrying a coffin on their shoulders together.

Then, those ineffable words of the Koran
burn the truth of life, with live voice
that warm their heart,
hotter than heat of the equator.

Above a forest shaded
over a low window,
One cold star is falling on their head.

---

* This poem was published in daily English newspaper, 'Indonesia Times' in 1984

삶의 진실을 불사르고
얕은 창 너머
그늘 이룬 숲 위로
찬 별 하나 떨어져 내린다.

---

* '이슬람의 삼일제'는 'For the soul of dead' 라는 제목으로 1984년 'Indonesia
  Times' 에 게재됨.

Story of a Strange Island Country

- in Singapore

The top of a hill where the sounds of birds,
like morning dewdrops
remain for a while, echoing,
hanging for a moment on tree branches.
Sunlight as white as a dove's wings.

The city of moulding,
brought about and dipping its feet
at the tip of the Strait of Malacca.
A fascinating country that,
when sucked into a jumbo jet,
travellers become yet another mold.

The country where peace prevailing
under strict rules, though the people gathered from
each different bloodlines.

Those who advance ahead of all others
to defend by themselves, childlike boy soldiers
sweat heavily in the jungle across the strait.
The girls, on the frontlines of life's battlefield
to realize dreams of my car, my home, sometimes
become shrewd like serpents,
The weariness, stacked in the vicinity
of a forest of buildings, is relieved

이상한 섬나라 이야기
- 싱가폴에서

아침이슬 머물다 가듯
새소리 잠시 나뭇가지에 걸려
우짖는 언덕바지
햇살은 비둘기 날개같이 희디희다.

말라카 격전지激戰地에
발끝 담그고 이룩한 조형造型의 도시
점보기 따라 빨려 들면
여행자 또한 하나의 조형이 되는
신기의 나라.

제각기 다른 핏줄로 모였으나
평화의 견고한 각질角質로 다스려지는 나라.

홀로 앞서가는 자,
스스로를 지키고자
앳된 소년병들은 해협 너머 정글 속에서
비지땀을 흘리고
마이홈 마이카 꿈을 위해
생활일선에 나선 처녀들은 뱀처럼 영악해지고
빌딩숲, 좁은 반경 속에서 쌓인 권태는
공원의 나무그늘아래서
후끈한 카섹스로 발산한다.

by hot car sex
under the shade of trees in the park.

An open cafe on a corner of the city center
where traffic is heavy.
The delicate sounds of a guitar
that smooth the old wrinkles of tourists
forgetting the night.
A Eurasian, wearing blue jeans,
holding a guitar like Yangheeun[*],
mixing <A traveler at a Seashore> by Nahoonah[*]
into his repertoire.
makes me realize once again
the human voice is the most beautiful sound
in the world.

Like the passing of morning dewdrops,
though travellers depart hurriedly,
the footsteps of countless other visitors
never cease…
This country that keeps living
as if riding on a cloud,
though prices rise
and hotels, shopping centers soar
like bamboo shoot.

Stars in the sky, stuck like a jewel
as bright as a pearl
over the equator, free of pollution.

---

* Yangheeun and Nahoonah: famous Korean singers

신호등 걸리는
도심 한 켠 오픈 카페
밤을 잊는 관광객들의 늙은 주름살 펴는 은은한 기타소리,
희은이 같은 통기타 청바지 혼혈아가
나훈아의 해변의 길손도 섞어 부르며
인간의 목소리야말로
세상에서 가장 아름답다는 걸
새삼 일깨워준다.

아침이슬 머물다가듯
여행자 서둘러 사라져도
끊이지 않고 찾아드는 무수한 발길들...
호텔, 쇼핑몰 죽순같이 치솟고
덩달아 물가가 뛰어올라도
구름 타듯 삶을 영위하는 나라.

보석처럼 박힌 하늘의 별
공해 없는 적도赤道 위에서 진주처럼 영롱하다.

At the Strait of Malacca

The end of Malay Peninsula
where blackish-blue currents lick
the reclaimed Prautecong land
tickling its newly formed flesh.

Singapore, a nightless city, illuminates
the ridges and furrows of waves,
as bright as the light
as if a cruise ship soon to leave,
and radiates the mood
of the southern country.
It is distant world in our eyes,
wandering workers,
still unable to overcome poverty....

Our only reassurance defending us,
comes from the thumping
of an enormous dredging vessel
pumping sand, our hearts
when, completed night's work,
sit on the deck, drinking soju,
Korean distilled liquor.

As if breaking the monotonous sound of insects,
the digging of lizards in the jungle, the cries of apes
spewing dense heat of a primary color,
ripens little by little.
Then, brilliant constellations

말라카 해협에서

검푸른 해류海流
프라우테콩 매립지를
새살 돋는 간지러움으로 핥는
말레이 반도의 끝

불야성不夜城 이룬 싱가폴은
출항 앞둔 유람선
은성한 불빛처럼 파도이랑 얼비치며
남국南國의 정취를 한껏 방사하고
아직도 가난의 허물 벗지 못해
떠도는 노가다판 우리네 가슴엔
별천지別天地 세계일 뿐...

야간작업을 끝내고
소주잔 기울이며 퍼질러 앉은
우리의 심장
쿵쿵 울려주는
저 거대한 준설선浚渫船 모래 펌프질만이
우리를 지켜주는 든든함이다.

풀벌레소리 단조로움 깨듯
정글을 헤집는 도마뱀, 잔나비 울음소리
원색의 짙은 열기 토해내며
시나브로 여물어가면

that spread at midnight,
our only consolation, touching tenderly
our drunken eyes.

Ghosts of young Koreans,
dragged from afar
at the period of our fathers
during the Pacific War, and were killed
like dogs at the height in their youth.

Unable to find a resting place,
did they wander about and finally
to take their places as constellations in the night sky?
while the waves washing their pure souls...

Around an observation post
with collapsed mud walls
A cannon shell, unexpectedly appearing
at the entrance of jungle
from where road construction is underway.
Removing obstacles lying in ambush here and there,
work at jobsites are on-going.

However, whenever we wash our mind
with waves of the night
our heart, too desolate to be comforted,
the sound of a torpedo,
still unexploded
entangled more and more inwards,
cries a vindictive spirit
strike the rim of our ear
like an audible ringing.

자시子時에 펼쳐지는 찬란한 성좌星座
우리의 취한 눈 어루만져 주는
유일한 위안이었다.

남태평양전쟁南太平洋戰爭때 끌려와
개죽음당한 아버지적 푸르디푸른
청춘의 망령亡靈들
어디에도 묻히지 못하고 떠돌다
저렇듯 밤하늘 별자리로 자리 잡은 것일까...
맑은 영혼 파도자락에 씻기우며.

흙담 무너져 내린 초소 언저리,
길을 뚫는 정글 입구에
불쑥 드러나는 포탄砲彈,
곳곳에 도사린 복병伏兵들을 제거하며
현장의 공정工程은 전진해 가지만

이따금
풀래야 풀 길 없는
우리의 적막한 가슴
밤 파도에 헹궈낼 때면
상기도 터지지 않고
안으로 안으로 엉킨 원혼冤魂을 우는 어뢰 울음소리
이명耳鳴처럼 귓전을 때린다.

On a Mountain

From the mountain peak
to the end of Central Java,
a flower that blooms
as if a grain of red passion,
over swaying leaves of asparagus.

Oh, Bituraden, lofty fortress!
You expel far below your feet
the surface heat
and nauseating smell of flesh,

Standing high, commanding fir trees,
always surrounded by clouds,
you bring raging billows at sunset
splitting the crown atop of sky
with raging wind, thunderstorm,
and are suddenly locked away
in pouring waterfall rain.

When day breaks,
morning glories welcome
the peace of forest
when birds sing all kinds song,
weather vanes clinging

산상山上에서

센트럴 자바의 끝점
아스파라가스 하늘대는 잎새 위
붉은 열정熱情의 입자粒子인 양 피어난 꽃.

살 내음 역겨운 지상의 열기
발치아래 내몰고
우뚝 전나무군群 거느리고
늘상 구름밭에 싸여
해질녘이면 하늘의 노도怒濤 몰고 와
광풍뇌우狂風雷雨로 하늘 정수리를 쪼개는,
그리하여 홀연히 비의 폭포 속에
갇히는 고고한 성채, 바뚜라덴이여!

날이 밝으면
온갖 잡새 우짖는 숲의 평화
낯익은 나팔꽃도 반기고
대나무 끝에 매달린 풍향계는
구름밭 위
새로이 열린 하늘 향해
새, 바람, 물소리 어우러진
청아한 음音의 합주를 이끌어낸다.

활화산活火山이 끓인 온천을 배회하는
바람보다 투명한 잠자리떼의 원무圓舞

to the end of bamboo tree,

over clouds
toward freshly opened skies,
bring out a concert of ringing sounds,
intermingle birds, wind, water and all others.

The circle dance of dragonflies
more transparent than the wind
hovering over the hot spring
boiled by an active volcano.

Standing at the entrance of a mountain village,
frog chorus, noisy enough
to shake the axis of earth.

Irresistible temptation in finding
something familiar at unfamiliar place...

As I went down the road
leading me again to the mundane world,
Baturaden, you hid yourself in foggy rain
and, despite the intense love affair between soul,
between you and me last night,
you did not even utter a farewell to me.

Oh, my Baturaden, cold, careless... Baturaden!

산마을 어귀에 내려서면
지축地軸 울리듯 시끌벅적한 개구리 합창,
낯선 곳에서 낯설지 않은 그 무엇을
찾아내고 이끌리는 알 수 없는 유혹.

다시 세속世俗의 길을 내려설 때
바뚜라덴, 너는 안개비에 스스로를 감추고
간밤 너와 가졌던 격렬했던 혼魂의 정사情事는 아랑곳없이
한 마디 이별의 말조차 없었다.

무심한, 무심한 나의 바뚜라덴이여.

Vicinity of an Active Volcano

- On the Mountain Tangkuban Perabu, Bandung, Indonesia

The narrow jungle path
leading to an active volcano.
Even mountain birds, trembling in fear,
hide themselves far away,
and anxiously cry as if to warn me,
whose steps are light, fearless:
Stop! Go no further!

Temptation of the other world
where poisonous sulfuric gas,
passing through the earth's crust,
emits at will.
The nearer I approach,
the shadow of death grows thicker
on the bark of black trees.

In the shades of high palm trees, coconuts beaming,
a troop of monkeys, many in number,
quicken their pace in a great hurry,
erasing their traces

Absolute desolation that causes even the wind,
halted between scattered leaves,
to hold its breath,

활화산 부근

- 인도네시아 반둥 Tankuban Perahu 산상에서

산새조차 두려움에 떨며
멀리 숨어 깃을 사리고
성큼 내닫는 겁 없는 나의 발길
거두라, 거두라 애탄 듯 울어예는
활화산 접어드는
정글속 소롯길.

유황 머금은 독가스
지각을 뚫고 무시로 치솟는
저 세상의 유혹,
다가가면 갈수록
검은 수목의 표피에 드리운
죽음의 그림자.

높은 야자그늘 코코넛 벙글듯
흔티 흔턴 잔나비떼
잰걸음 서둘러 흔적을 지우고

성긴 잎새에 머문 바람조차
시간의 덫에 채여
숨죽인 절대적막絕對寂寞...

마침내 감전感電되듯
소름끼치며 만나는

having fallen into the trap of time....
Then I meet, at last,
hairs raised as if electrocuted,
Genesis chapter one, line one

Oh! The magic lamp of Aladdin,
quick to rise
over the time machine back to ancient times.

The deceased souls
wail, boiling out from every gap
of a seething heart.
Their incomprehensible shouting
collectively raising their voices,

When a fossilized bird
from a crack in the limestone
soars into the sky, wrapped in smoke,
as if coming back to life,

I also transform into the Cromagnon
in my distant memory by throwing away
awkward veil of civilization.

창세기 1장 1절

오,
반전하는 드라마의 한 폭처럼
고대의 타임 마신 위에
솟구쳐 오르는 알라딘의 요술램프.

들끓는 심장 터진 틈새마다
비등沸騰하며 울부짖는 사자死者의 정령精靈들
함께 목청 돋우어
살아 아우성치는 불가해한 함성.

석회암 균열된 어디쯤선가
음각陰刻된 새의 화석化石
부활하듯 연막에 싸여
하늘을 오르면

나 또한 변신한
먼 기억속의 끄레마뇽인人
어설픈 문명의 너울 벗어 던진다.

Jungle

Oh, you!
Embracing an infinitely large number of things,
fresh thoughts, never decaying,
wander about with your burning heart.
Tangled, entangled, and knotted,
you tie yourself with your own hands
and flop to the ground.

Oh, you!
You open your inner eyes for the first time
and raise your scraped, bruised kneecaps
while, in the abandoned shade,
locked in the darkness, cut off even from daylight,
you govern and carve into, silently,
a grudging heart
the sharp passing of time, the raging winds
that cruelly whip your bare back.

Oh, you!
Your large motions as you once again rise
disentangle, little by little, the knots
tied so tightly, and in every small space created
lies a path for all animals and birds,
opening the ground and sky

정글

한량없이 많은 것 보듬고
결코 썩지 않는 풋풋한 사유思惟
타는 가슴으로 헤매이다
얽히고 뒤얽히고 매듭지어져
스스로를 묶고 주저앉은 그대여.

버림받은 음지
날빛마저 차단된 어둠에 갇혀
벗겨진 등짝
몰아 때리는 광풍狂風의 시련, 모진 세월
웅어리진 가슴으로
묵묵히 새기며 다스리다가
비로소 내면의 눈을 뜨고
상처 난 무릎 끝을 세우는 그대.

그대 다시 일어서는 거대한 몸짓에
결결이 맺힌 매듭 조금씩 풀리며
트여오는 공간마다
뭇 짐승, 날 것들의 길을 만들어
그들만의 땅과 하늘을 열어 놓곤
썩은 칡넝쿨, 낙엽더미에 주저앉아
아직도 태고太古를 향해 등 돌리고 앉은
그대여.

just for them.
Then, plopping down on the rotten arrowroot vines
and heaps of fallen leaves,
you still face time immemorial, back turned.

Embracing the souls of even abandoned human being,
you dream of the sky
when the road for them will be opened wide,
but I know it is still far, far away.

버림받은 인간의 혼魂마저 보듬어
그들의 길 열어놓을 때 다가올
그대 꿈꾸는 하늘은
아직도 멀리 있음을 나는 안다.

To Batak* Brothers

Though only two have gathered,
they attune their harmonies,
When three have gathered,
they pluck their guitar strings.

Their hearts, a deep fountain of songs,
are always overflowing a concert of delight.

The mountain peak that rises high,
carrying atop its head the northwestern sky
of Sumatra, Indonesia.
And romantic folk songs
that ring over the mountainside,
tearing up the morning mist
spreads, like the incantation of an active volcano,
over the surface of Lake Toba
as wide as an ocean.

Carrying on their backs, like karmic suffering,
shabby sacks of poverty,
they aim to pillars of fire
soaring over the heads of palm trees,
heading to construction yard.
Their needy-looking rags,
purposely pacified with raised laughter
as they harmonize with do, sol, la, si, sol.

바딱 형제들에게

그들은 둘만 모여도
화음을 맞추고
셋이 되면 기타 줄을 튕긴다.

가슴은 깊디깊은 노래의 샘,
늘 차고 넘치는 흥겨움의 합주合奏.

인도네시아 수마트라
서북西北 하늘이고 우뚝 솟은 산정山頂
큰 바다 같이 펼쳐진 레익토바Lake Toba 호면湖面을
활화산의 주문呪文처럼 번지는
아침안개 헤집고
산허리를 울리는 낭만의 노랫가락.

초라한 가난의 행낭
업고業苦처럼 지고
야자수 너머 치솟는 불기둥 표적삼아
공사판 찾아 나선 그들,
궁기 낀 헐벗음
뒷박 웃음으로 짐짓 눙쳐버리고
도솔라시솔 화음和音 이뤄 목청 돋운다.

10억불 호화판 정유공장 프로젝트에서도
그들의 몫은 고작 허드레 잡일뿐

Even in lavish oil refinery project
amounting one billion dollars,
their lots are given only trifling jobs.
A harsh and arduous life.
A meager life that continues without even pillows
for them to lay their heads on to breathe easily.

Nevertheless, on a fete day,
they become kings on the stage.

They play the lead role in a pierrot-like life
where a beggar prince becomes a prince.
And expressing the joy and anger with the sorrow and pleasure
of human lives,
sometimes with comedy
sometimes like thunder and light ening,
they frolic and roar
making audiences laugh and weep,
draw out the deeply moved applause.

Their harmonic voices, diminishing quietly,
become, at last, the sound of rain
falling on the vast Lake Toba,
awakening men of the root of sorrow,
enlightening them to the true meaning
of human nature, treasured more richly
in the heart of the poor,
Afer all, turn into a long, rushing river.

---

* Batak : located nearby Great big Lake called 'Lake Toba' in Sumatra, Indonesia

고되고 거친 삶
숨 고르고 누울 베개조차 없는
척박한 삶의 연속이지만

축제일祝祭日이면 그들은
무대의 왕王이 된다.

거지왕자가 왕자가 되는
피에로 같은 생의 주역主役이 되고
삶이 주는 희비애락喜悲哀樂을
때로는 코미디로,
때로는 뇌성벽력으로
짓까불다간 포효하며
웃기고 울리다가
끝내는 감동의 박수를 이끌어낸다.

이윽고 잔잔히 잦아드는
그들의 화음은
드넓은 레익 토바를 적시는 빗소리 되어
슬픔의 근원을 알려주고
가난한 자에게 더욱 풍요로이 간직된
인정人情의 참뜻 일깨워주며
도도히 흐르는 장강長江이 된다.

---

* 바딱 : 인도네시아 수마트라'대륙 속의 바다'로 불리는 토바(Toba) 호(湖) 인근 지역으로
  예인(藝人)들이 많이 배출되는 곳으로 유명하다

To Eric Pical,
IBF Junior Bantham Champion

Eric Pical, at last,
you step into the ring,
with dark red muscle cooked
by boiling heat of the equator,
like the image of an African native,
your face imbued with
shade of the Third World.

The moist enthusiasm of frenzied Jakartans.
Their glittering eyes, yearning
to see World Champion for their own.
All eyes focused on the ring
illuminated by dazzling spotlight.

Even though it was not WBA or WBC title match
but a fledgling IBF title,
it was really overwhelming challenge for Indonesia,
having never ascended to top of the world.

However, it would be the substance of hope,
seeming to be almost within grasp.

Audience still remembers.
Middle-weight boxer, their hero,
raised by Ache on the northern tip of Sumatra,

IBF 주니어 밴텀급 챔피언 에릭 피칼에게

적도赤道의 뜨거운 열기에 구워진
검붉은 근육,
아프리카토족土族의 형상이
제3세계의 그늘같이 스민 얼굴로
에릭 피칼,
너는 마침내 링에 올랐다.

열광하는 자카르타 시민의 습한 열기熱氣,
세계 챔피언을 저의 것으로 만들고자 하는
갈망의 눈빛, 눈빛들이 일제히
스포트라이트 눈부신 링 위로 꽂혔다.

WBA, WBC 타이틀매치가 아닌
신생新生 IBF타이틀전이나
단 한 번도 세계 정상에 올라본 적이 없는
남국의 나라, 인도네시아로선
가슴 벅찬 도전이었다.

그러나 손으로 잡을 수 있을 것도 같은
희망의 실체實體이기도 했다.

관중들은 기억하고 있다.
수마트라 북쪽 끝 아체가 키운
미들급 복서 영웅이

shattered their dream to pieces
and disappeared like a bubble
under the strong punch of Korean...

Korea, the country in Far East,
racing far ahead of Indonesia
with its flourishing economic growth.
Though alike as Asians,
they do not know the sorrow of black skin,
theirs being white, clear, clean and beautiful.

They were the object of envy,
near but distant.
They crisscrossed the ground of Southeast Asia
with their white, sturdy, iron legs,
making new road deep into native jungles,
building oil refineries that shined
with imposing silvery grand appearance.

Luxurious Benz cars rush down the jungle road,
and Toyotas speedily run along their own street,
but they, Indonesians, still pulling rickshaws,
a stoic country
that must be content
with life on the bottom rung.

Rich and beautiful nature,
fiery pillars of black gold
gushing from the tranquil sea,

그들의 기대를 산산조각내고
한국의 강펀치에 물거품으로 사라져간 것을...

눈부신 경제성장으로
저만큼 앞서 달리는 극동의 나라,
한국 같은 아세아족族이나
그들에겐 검은 피부의 설움이 없었으며
희고 맑고 깨끗하고 아름다웠다.

가깝고도 먼 부러움의 대상이었다.

그들은 희고 튼튼한 건각으로
동남아의 론 그라운드를 누볐으며
고향 정글 깊숙이 길을 뚫고
은빛 위용 번쩍이는 정유공장을 만들어내기도 했다.

뚫린 길을 치달리는 호화판 벤츠차와
도요다가 저들의 거리를 질주하나
아직도 저들은 빼차나 끌며
바닥의 생활을 자족해야 하는 인고忍苦의 나라.

풍요롭고 아름다운 자연,
고요한 바다에서 뿜어 나오는
검은 황금의 불기둥도
아직은 저희 것이 될 수 없는
서러운 땅의 한 젊은이가
맨 주먹 하나로
세계 정상을 넘보며

could not yet be possessed by them.
One bare young man of this sad land,
with only his bare fist,
willing to reach top of the world
and rolling like a wave,
dashed into round after round.

Sheet! Sheet!
The short wind
slices the air sharply
like the blade of knife.
Sometimes striking at the jaw of champion,
Jeon Judo, with no concern for
ungentlemanly violation
if hitting the handsome face of champion,
while clinching.

Carrying on your back
150 million commoners,
who, hidden under the shadow of generals,
oppressed by the maldistribution of wealth,
had become thin, suffered illness,
Eric Pical! you aimed for a point of advantage
like a hunter laying a snare,
pausing, never hurrying.

It finally happened in a flash.
His left fist split the wind,
evading the charge of the impatient champion,

파도같이 일렁이며
라운드, 라운드를 대쉬해 들어갔다.

쉬잇 쉿 칼날같이 맵차게
허공을 가르는 짧은 바람
이따금 챔피언 전주도의 턱을 깨며
클린치한 채
핸섬한 챔피언의 얼굴을 때리는
비신사적인 반칙도 마다않고

장군들의 그늘에 가려
부富의 편재에 눌려
야위고 병들어가야 했던
1억 5천만 서민을 등에 업고
에릭 피칼, 너는 덫을 놓은 사냥꾼같이
길목을 노리며 뜸을 들였다.
결코 서두르지 않았다.

일순간이었다.
초조해진 챔피언의 돌진을 피하며
바람을 가른 왼쪽 주먹
그것은 보이지 않을 만큼 빨랐고 또 정확했다.
챔피언은 매트에 머리를 부딪치며
나뒹굴었다. 치명적인 주먹이었다.

원화의 평가절하
루피아의 평가절상

it was invisibly quick, also precise.
Head knocking against mat,
the champion tumbled down.
Eric's fist was fatal.

Devaluation of Won.
Upward revaluation of Rupiah.

The audience, shouting for joy
like pouring water from a broken dam.
The birth of new champion
being carried on the shoulders of men.

At that time I saw!

The true character of new champion
embracing his beggared, old mother,
weeping together.
I found the naked figure of Eric Pical,
the long-lived sorrow hidden
behind his sound face revealing itself,
wailing wildly like a beast.

It was the beautiful nature
representing Third World's people,
resembling the primitive man of Java.

터진 봇물처럼 환호하는 관중
무등 탄 새 챔피언의 탄생.

그 때 나는 보았다.

가난의 궁기 낀 늙은 어머니를 포옹하며 함께 우는
챔피언의 참모습을,
온전한 제 얼굴 속에 감춰졌던
오랜 서러움의 정체를 한껏 드러내고
짐승처럼 울부짖는
에릭 피칼의 적나라한 모습을.

그것은 자바원인의 원시성을 닮은
제3세계 서민의 아름다운 본성이었다.

Cowboy Party

From a welder of 19 years old
to supervisor, 30 years,
having worked on construction sites
at every corner of the world.
Mr. Cox, my dear friend, was a soldier
who had participated in Korean War.

Bald like the actor Yule Brynner.
Boots never free of muddy soils
from the construction site.
He always shows off his diligence.
We call him Mr. Fox behind his back,
as his skillful conduct in life, sometimes,
looking even a bit cunning.

His wife says without hesitation
that he loves work more than her.
Her grandmother was Chinese, so she,
now a silver-haired grandmother,
reveals Oriental virtues.

Before her dignified composure
even Mr. Cox cannot help
but be a helpless child.
His sole source of pride

카우보이 파티

열아홉 살 때부터 용접공으로 출발하여
감독관이 되기까지
30여년 지구촌 구석구석
건설현장 헤집고 다닌 나의 친구
Mr. Cox,
그는 6.25 때 참전용사였다.

율브리너 같은 대머리에
현장의 뻘흙 장화에서 마를 날 없는
부지런 떠는 그를
우리는 뒷전에서 Mr. Fox로 불러댔다.

노련한 그의 처세는
약간의 교활성마저 엿보였으므로.

자기보다 일을 더 사랑한다고
서슴없이 말하는 그의 부인은
조모祖母때 중국계 피를 이어받아
약간의 동양적 미덕도 엿보이는
은발의 할머니.

그녀의 의젓함 앞에 Mr. Cox도 별 수 없는 어린애였다.
대물린 동양의 피 섞임은
Mr. Cox의 은근한 자랑거리였다.

being his family pedigree
mixed with Oriental blood.

Today Mr. and Mrs. Cox have placed
slabs of meat as ample as a horse's buttock
on a grill over dry firewood, flames rising,
and open the whole, inside and outside, of their house.
Today is the day of their exciting party,
so called "Cowboy Party."

Everyone wears a smart cowboy hat,
some leather jackets.
Spanish women wear clothes
that seem to spontaneously burst
into flamenco dance.
Each sending forth, to one end, the smell
of cowboys from the pioneer West,
a throng of people gathers clamorously.

Asking a favor of any woman, I tied around my neck
a handkerchief stained with perfume,
together talking, drinking, bodies shaking.
sometimes with a "ee-hee-hee-hee!"
a curious noise like that of the trio Los Panchos,
spreads across the tropical jungle.
Truly a pleasant evening.

A skinny man in a Mexican cape
and broad-brimmed hat,

오늘 Mr. Cox 부부는
말 엉덩이짝만큼 푸짐한 고깃덩어리
마른 장작 훨훨 화력 돋우는
석쇠 위에 올려놓고
집 안팎 온통 열어젖히고
흥거운 파트를 열었다.
이름하여 '카우보이 파티'

날렵한 카우보이모자, 더러는 가죽 재킷,
스페인 여자는 플라밍고 춤 맵시
절로 일 듯한 의상 차려입고
저마다 서부개척시대 카우보이 냄새
어느 한 켠에 풍기며
시끌벅적 모여든 무리들.

아무 여자에게나 부탁해
향후 묻은 손수건 목에 감아 걸고
함께 떠들고 마시고 뒤흔들다
이따금씩 이히히히—
트리오 로스 판초스 같은 기성奇聲,
열대의 정글로 번져 나가는
유쾌한 저녁 한때.

멕시코 망토에 창 넓은 모자 쓴
삐쩍 마른 사내와
방구들 꺼질 듯 벌어진 여자가
여흥의 불꽃 심지 한껏 돋우는
파티의 하이라이트.

and woman wide enough
to crush the wooden floor
set ablaze the entertainment to a climax
as party's highlight.

Lower part of bodies
being appropriately indecent together,
upper part of the body
moderately classy,
approaching close, then parting…
A spell of excited dancing
flushed amid cheers and applause.

The western lass who handed over to me
her handkerchief, embraces her stepfather,
as if her lover, to her large breast
begins to spin.

During which one of our colleagues
goes out stealthily and urinates,
looking up at the countless stars
falling down from the darkened sky.

Leaving behind his family in Korea
swallowing alone his solitude,
his back is weighed down
by desolateness.

My heart unexpectedly begins to chill...

하체끼리 적당히 외설적으로
또 상체끼리 적당히 품위 있게
가까워졌다 멀어졌다...
환호와 박수 속에 상기된 한바탕 춤가락.

네게 손수건을 건네 준 서양계집은
제 의붓아비를 애인인양
유방 큰 가슴으로 껴안고 도는 와중에

우리 일행 중 누군가
슬몃 빠져나가
거뭇한 하늘 쏟아지는 뭇별들
하염없이 치어다보며
방뇨를 하고 있다.

일가붙이 두고 홀로 쓸쓸함을 삭이는
그의 등짝에 내리깔리는 적막.

문득 가슴이 서늘히 식어온다.

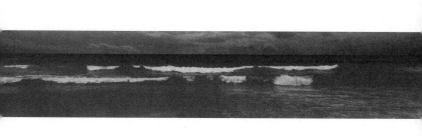

제3부 바다

Part Three The Sea

Impression of the Aegean Sea

The space of imagination
without limit.

As if born from the deep
and cozy wombs of our mothers,
you are the great source
of humankind's culture.

The clear wind blowing
from the Ionia Sea always
excites our steps,
while we prepare our dream.

These squirming muscles
that hoist sails for departure,
waiting for the wind to rise.

Our lives are happy
as long as we proceed towards you.

On top of the mast hanging
the lofty ideal and hope
that could not be hoisted from the ground,
The long voyage of Odyssey

에게해 인상

가없는 상상력의 공간.

깊고 아늑한 어머니의 자궁 속에서
우리들이 잉태하듯
그대는
위대한 인류문화의 근원.

이오니아바다로부터
불어오는 해맑은 바람은
꿈을 예비하는 우리들의 발길
늘상 설레게 하고

바람이 일기를 기다려
출범의 돛을 올리는
이 근육의 꿈틀거림.

그대를 향해 나아가는
우리들의 삶은 행복하여라.

마스트 끝에는
지상에서 건져 올리지 못한
높은 이상과 희망을 달고
형상화되지 못한 그 모든 그리움의 실체를 찾아 떠나는
오디세이의 긴 항해航海.

in search of the substance of all their longing,
those that failed to be realized.

The silvery sea that swells
with the rising sun.
Its rising, high waves, a challenge
as sharp as a knifeblade.
Our dreams press forward vigorously
beating the ship's bow.

The challenge of high waves
ripens our dream more and more.
The muse who whispers like a breeze,
the sound of your song also endless
the sadness of our lives
is without end as well.

Your face elucidates our lives,
reflecting more transparently
than a mirror.

Our lives are happy
as long as we proceed towards you,

Though our voyage may, at last,
end with nets cast pursuing dream
in immeasurable loneliness…

떠오르는 해와 함께
출렁이는 은빛바다,
파도이랑 세우는 칼날 선 도전
뱃머리를 으깨이며
힘차게 전진하는
우리 모두의 꿈,

파고 높은 도전이 있기에
우리들의 꿈 더욱 영글어가고
미풍처럼 속살거리는
뮤즈, 그대 노래소리는
끝이 없고
인생의 슬픔 또한 끝이 없어라.

우리들의 삶을 명징하게
거울보다 투명하게 비춰주는
그대의 얼굴,

그대를 향해 나아가는
우리들의 삶은 행복하여라.

비록 우리들이 항해가
바없는 외로움 속에
꿈의 투망질에 그친다 할지라도...

Monologue of
a Salmon in Namdaechon River

Yellow eyes devoid of focus,
mouths without muscle function,
fins that follow the stream inertly,
lifeless water plants
that float up to surface murkily....

Unable to proceed further
against the flow of Namdaechon River,
salmons are drifting.
One after another, they come up
to the surface like disused spaceships
discarded in a state of zero gravity.

The course of their journey covered
half the world,
travelling without rest
from the end of the North Pacific,
through the Kamchaka Peninsula and Hokkaido Island,
crossing the ceasefire line of tragedy,
and shrewdly working through the jumble
of cold and warm currents.

The motherland at which they arrived, at last,
after a long fight for survival,

남대천 연어의 독백

초점 잃은 노란 눈
근육기능이 상실된 입,
물살 따라 관성처럼 내맡겨진 지느러미,
뿌옇게 떠오르는 생기 잃은 물풀들...

더 이상 남대천 상류를 거스르지 못하고
부유하는 연어들
무중력 상태에 버려진 폐우주선처럼
하나, 둘 떠오르고 있습니다.

저 북태평양 끝에서
캄차카반도, 북해도를 거쳐
비극의 휴전선을 넘어
한류와 난류의 뒤엉킴 지혜롭게 헤쳐
지구 반 바퀴를 쉼없이 돌아온 여정旅程

끝없이 움직이며
쉴 새 없이 지느러미를 흔들며
돌고래, 상어, 감성돔 때로는 말미잘 숲을 용케 빠져나와
예까지 이르른 생존의 긴 투쟁 끝
마침내 와 닿은 어머니의 땅.

태어날 적 단 한번 느꼈던
남대천의 차디차나 상쾌했던 세찬 물살

moving ceaselessly,
shaking their fins nonstop,
skillfully escaping
dolphins, sharks, black porgies,
and forests of sea anemones.

That which they felt only once, at birth,
the icy, refreshing, strong currents of Namdaecheon
at the ends of their scales, as if by instinct.
But before they feel it, rapturously, with their bodies,
from some estuary where the East Sea
and downstreams of Namdaecheon mix,
an overpowering stench, floating debris
that completely obstruct their vision,
and suffocation as if their chests
were being squeezed…

Oh, God Almighty!
Without the chance to give birth
to the countless seeds of life you gave me...
to welcome the joy of spawning my beloved selves
to swim the vast Pacific Ocean,
yet unable to taste
the tired yet full
and peaceful death following labor…

Oh, God Almighty!
Why do you abandon me!

본능처럼 비늘 끝에, 온 몸으로 황홀하게 느끼기도 전에
동해바다와 남대천 하류가 몸을 섞는
어느 어귀에선가
숨 막히는 악취,
앞을 볼 수 없는 탁한 부유물
가슴을 죄어오는 숨 막힘...

오, 하느님!
당신이 주신 이 수많은 생명의 씨앗
낳아보지도 못하고
사랑하는 나의 분신들 저 너른 태평양 바다
마음껏 유영하는 산란의 기쁨 속에 맞이할,
진통 끝의 나른하나 충만하고 안온한 죽음
맛보지도 못하고...

오! 하느님
왜 저를 버리시나이까!

Sea is Uneasy

The migration of soul
which cannot be stopped,
though repeating endlessly.

Yet you adamantly refuse
to stand still, always carrying
free, boundless wind
and raising wild wave.

Your relentless passion
borrowing the attraction of duel cosmic force,
heavy, clumsy moon and hot sun.
Where will it rest?

Water flowing down valley
covered by permanent snow and ice
wets the Hindustan Plain,
Rocky Mountains, Grand Canyon,
as well as the sad legend of Colorado Indians,

Upon belching out
unending cries from the river's mouth,
the river defends itself,
filtering the shame stained by civilization.

바다는 불안하다

돌고 돌아도
멈출 수 없는 윤회

그래도 한사코 머무름을 거부하는,
항시 무변無邊의 자유로운 바람 싣고
거친 파도 일으키며

둔중한 달과 뜨거운 해
음양陰陽의 인력引力을 빌어
감출 길 없는 그대 열정
머물 곳은 어디런가.

만년설 얼음 골짜기
흘러내린 물 힌두스탄 평야를 적시고
록키산맥 그랜드 캐니언
콜로라도 인디언 슬픈 전설을 적시며

강 하구마다
질펀한 울음 한바탕 토해낸 후
문명文明에 더럽혀진 오욕汚辱 걸러내
스스로를 지키던 바다.

오늘 그 바다가
오존층 구멍 뚫고 무방비로 퍼붓는 직사광선에

Today, the sea is writhing with a high fever
from direct rays of light
mercilessly pouring down
through holes in the ozone layer.

The sea's birth, death, and rebirth,
Somehow uneasy
trying to escape its cycle.

By resisting earth's rotation,
the tangle of currents, the rule of submitting itself,
struggles to recover
sublime soul of its stream.

Oh! magnificent whirlpool,
drawing an immense circle reaching 300km,
swells as if even the vast sea were narrow.

Dreadful sea storm makes
even the fishes in vast sea shudder,
with its terrible gusts as fast as thunder
flying around 140km per hour,
almost ready to push away a continent.
Measuring instrument of satellite
madly shaking in outer space.

The revolt of sea,
at last, starts.

신열身熱로 달떠 몸부림치고 있다.
원심으로부터 벗어나려는
왠지 불안한 바다의 윤회.

바다는 지구의 자전自轉
해류의 뒤엉킴에
스스로를 맡기는 순리順理를 거스르며
저 웅혼한 흐름의 넋
되찾으려 몸부림친다.

300km 거대한 원을 그리며
대양大洋마저 좁은 듯 굽이치는
장엄한 소용돌이.

대륙을 밀어낼 듯
시속 140km 광속구光速球의 무서운 치달음으로
적막한 바다 속 고기마저 떨게 하는 바다폭풍.
인공위성 판독기가 우주공간에서 뒤흔들리고 있다.

마침내 일어나는 바다의 반란.

A Butterfly Having a Merry Time Around the Manmulsang Rocks of the East Sea

Past Myungpari,
over the civilian passage restriction line,
through Geojin and Gansung,
towns at north end of National Road no. 7,
and having climbed Geonbong Mountain
shrouded in clouds and mist,
looking as lonely as an island,
lies Namgang River,
traversing the dense, wooded demilitarized zone
flows into the East Sea.

Only peace overflows
as if forgotten in those days 48 years ago,
the bloody massacre that swept across,
had been cleansed away completely.
Yet when a soldier, logging, has an occasion
to wash the perspiration from his face
at the river's edge, bullets fly at him, without fail,
from a bunker shaded by the forest.

The area near Namgang River
Is swathed in tension as sharp
as the sunlight reflecting on flowing stream.

동해바다 만물상에 노니는 나비 한 마리

7번국도 북단 끝
거진 간성 거쳐
민통선 마을 명파리 지나
늘상 구름 안개 거닐고 있어
섬처럼 외로운 건봉산에 오르면
녹음 짙은 비무장지대 한복판을
동해로 흘러가는 남강南江이 가로지르고 있다.

피의 살육 흥건했던
48년 전 역사 죄다 씻긴 듯 평화만 가득하나
어쩌다
벌목 작업하던 병사가 강가에 땀이라도 씻을라치면
숲속 그늘진 방카에서
어김없이 날아오는 총알.

남강 주변은 늘상
강물에 반사하는 햇살만큼
팽팽한 긴장이 감돈다.

그래도 비극의 인간사를 아는지
무심한 남강은 유유히
일만이천봉 금강산 계곡 맑은 물
죄다 입에 담아 해금강 어귀에 부려 놓는다.

Yet, as if aware of the tragic history,
the indifferent Namgang calmly gulps
clear water from the valleys of Diamond Mountain,
all twelve-thousand peaks
and unloads it at the mouth of Haegeumgang.

Manmulsang Rock, embracer of all earthly shapes,
those of whales, deer, rabbits, men,
protector of the door to the East Sea,
asked the Namgang River:
"Why do you draw water every day
to pour it on the top of our feet?"

The river answered:

"No amount of water poured
Will fully fill the East Sea,
And no amount of water drawn
Will dry it completely.*
Therefore, I like to play here
as I please."

Having heard their dialogue,
a butterfly of Zhuangzi is coming
from the end of the sea,
fluttering its wings lightly.

---

* "No amount of water poured ... will dry it completely." is quoted from the 'Heaven and Earth' chapter of a book by the ancient Chinese Philosopher, Zhuangzi.

고래, 사슴, 토끼, 인간 온갖 사바세계 형상 다 담은
만물상이 동해바다 문전을 지키다
남강에게 묻기를,
"왜 그대는 날마다 물을 길어 내 발등에 붓느냐?"하니

"동해는 아무리 물을 부어도 차지 않으며
아무리 물을 길어 내어도 마르지 않는다.*
그래서 나는 여기서 한껏 놀고자 하는 것이다."

그 대화를 듣고 저 바다 끝에서
나풀거리며 날아오는 장자의 나비 한 마리.

---

* '동해는 … 않는다': 장자(莊子)의 〈천지편〉에서 인용

Oryukdo Island

Did several brother whales,
coming to and from East Sea,
become curious about the human world
and wish to rest, for a while,
their tired bodies?

Five fins, on good terms,
lying side by side on the sea's surface,
sometimes six fins over the swelling waves
Your actual body, hidden, perhaps?

Having wandered day after day in foreign lands
since leaving Bangojin Port of Ulsan City,
famous for whaling in my childhood,
whales were objects of my longing,
to be seen from afar.
They were the substance of dream
to be fulfilled, going out into the world,
and were, rather, awe itself.

The coast of Busan, departing into the Pacific
Always laden with hopes of full catch,
Looking at islands that seem both near and far,
Floating atop surging waves,

오륙도

동해를 오가던 형제 고래 몇 마리
인간 세상사 궁금해
잠시 지친 몸 가누고 싶었던 것일까.

사이좋게 나란히 다섯 지느러미
수면 위에 드러내 놓고
때로는 넘실대는 파도 깃에 여섯 지느러미 내비치는
너의 감춰진 실체는 혹 거대한 흰긴수염고래는 아닐는지.

어릴 적 고래잡이로 유명했던
울산 방어진을 떠나 줄곧 타관을 떠돌았던 내게
고래는 늘 두고 바라보는 그리움의 대상이었다.
세상에 나아가 성취해야 할
꿈의 실체이자 경외로움 그 자체였다.

늘상 태평양으로 만선의 꿈을 안고 출항하는 부산 앞바다
넘실대는 파도 깃에 떠 있는
멈춘 듯 다가서고, 손짓하다 멈춘 듯한
멀고도 가까운 저 섬들을 바라보며
왜 고래고기맛과 함께 어린 시절
내 곁을 떠나버린 고래를 떠올렸을까.

거대한 숨구멍 벌름거릴 때마다
찬연히 허공에 흩뿌려지는 무지개빛,

Approaching while halted, halting while gesturing at us,
why did I recollect the whales
that had left me in my youth
along with the taste of whale meat?

The colors of a rainbow
that scatter in the air brilliantly
with the flaring
of the whale's huge nostrils.
The grand advance of the whale
like a mountain
jolting with its breathless diving.
The rebirth of splendid colors,
red, scarlet, yellow, green, blue, indigo, and violet,
towing me, a middle-aged man,
to the entrance of South Pacific,

It comes nearer irresistably, standing on its toes
toward the substance of splendid longing
even if I try to bury it under the waves.

숨찬 자맥질 따라 요동치는 산맥과도 같은 도도한 항진航進
그 화려한 빨, 주, 노, 초, 파, 남, 보 빛의 환생이
중년中年의 나를 견인해 남태평양 어귀로 이끌고 있다.

파도 깃에 묻어버리려 해도
한사코 발돋움하며 다가서는 찬연한 그리움의 실체로...

Coral Reef of the Equator

The moving, living, sculptured thing
that cannot live for a moment
in dirty sea,
takes root only in pure water,
swaying from side to side
only in peaceful mood, mild
subtropical climates over 25℃ degrees Celsius.

Content with plankton
among jellyfishes, hydras,
protozoa whose evolution has stopped,
they provide a resting place,
a gorgeous flower bed,
To clams, sea breams, urchins, starfish,
shrimp, crabs,
those weak and timid friends.

The group dance of coral reefs
nameless in the South Pacific,
calm like Debussy music
but a gentle, sweet routine,
overflowing with emotion
like Polynesian dance.

적도의 산호초

더러운 바다 속에서는
잠시도 살 수 없는,
청정한 바다에만
깃들여 뿌리 내리는
25℃ 이상 아열대성기후
평안 깃든 온화한 물결에서만
출렁이는 움직이는 조각.

해파리, 히드라
진화 멈춘 원생동물 사이에서
플랑크톤으로 자족自足하며
조개, 돔, 거미고동, 성게, 불가사리, 새우, 게
여리고 겁먹은 친구들에게
꽃밭 화사한 안식처를 마련해 주고

드뷔시 음악같이 잔잔하나
감미로운 율동
폴리네시아인 춤처럼
정감 넘치는
남태평양 이름 없는
산호초들의 군무群舞.

산호 깔린 석회암에서만
불꽃으로 활활 타오르는

Do you know that
only limestone covered with corals
can produce the oil of fiery passion
that burns vigorously, sending up flame?

정염의 석유가 나온다는 걸
그대는 아시는지?

Wrecked Sea

- The Spaceship Columbia Conducting the "Noah's Arc" Experi-
  ment, Carrying Animals, as if Considering the Day when Earth Is
  No More Inhabitable

Mountains of ice collapse,
groaning, flesh tearing away
piece by piece.
The Antarctic, split, is being wrecked.

The yellowish ozone layer where a hole has been bored.
Tropical rain forest aflame
Belts of pollution
floating over every city
Carbon dioxide is rapidly increasing.

Having lost the fresh, cool refreshment of purity,
the sea no longer kisses the good earth
with pure, genuine passion.

"Help me!
Seawater is rising up to my chin!
A sea monster incessantly tugs at my feet!"

The islands of South Pacific,
Paradise of Polynesian people,
are sinking.
The ground where I stand is sinking.

Boom! Bang!

난파당하는 바다

- 우주선 콜럼비아호가 동물들을 싣고 '노아의 방주' 실험을 하고 있다.
  더 이상 살 수 없을 지구를 미리 염두에 둔 듯

살 조각 떼어내듯
신음하며 무너져 내리는 얼음산
남극이 쪼개져 난파되고 있다.

구멍 뚫린 노오란 오존층
불타는 열대우림
도시마다 떠도는 공해띠
급증하는 이산화탄소

싱싱하고 차가운 순도純度의 상쾌함을 잃은 바다는
더 이상 순수한 열정으로 대지를 입맞춤하려 하지 않는다.

"살려주세요!
바닷물이 턱 끝까지 차오르고 있어요!
바다귀신이 발끝을 자꾸 당기고 있어요!"

폴리네시아인의 낙원
남태평양 섬들이 가라앉고 있다.
내가 선 땅이 침몰하고 있다.

우르르릉, 쾅!
한가로운 낮잠을 즐기던
바다표범, 펭귄 가족, 하얀 곰이 놀라

The seals, penguins and white bears
enjoying their leisurely siesta,
are startled, fall head over heels
diving into the sea.
A crowd of fur seals screams noisily.

The temperature of seawater
rose with a slight fever.
El Nino, which destroyed earth
with whirlpools, steps so wide
as to leap over five oceans and six continents.
The insomnia afflicting mankind,
Afflicts animals and the sea.

When the Antarctic Continent screamed in pain
as if healthy flesh being torn off,
a block of ice, larger than South Korea,
broke away.

The ghost of Titanic, trapped under 800 meters,
Invade the harbors of living men...

Tick! tick! tack! tack!, tick! tack! tack!...
Greenpeace headquarters dispatches
urgent distress calls in Morse code,
floated on today's internet screen.

The collapse of ice ridges will continue.
human conscience will also
continue to collapse.
Justice, vain ambition...
At last, the futile hope of men!

서둘러 바다 속으로 곤두박질치고 있다
물개떼가 꽥꽥꽥 아우성치고 있다.

미열을 넘어선 해수 온도,
5대양 6대주를 뛰어넘는
보폭 넓은 소용돌이로 지구를 파괴하는 엘니뇨
인간이 앓는 불면증을
동물이 앓고, 바다가 앓고 있다.

남극이 생살 떼어내는 아픔으로 비명을 지르자
남한 면적보다 넓은 얼음덩어리가 깨어져 나갔다.
두께 800m로 잠겨 인간의 항구로 쳐들어오는
타이타닉호의 유령들...

뚜뚜따따! 뚜따따!
모르스부호로 타전해 오던
그린피스 본부의 긴급구조 신호가
오늘은 인터넷 화면에 떠오른다.

빙벽의 붕괴는 계속될 것이다.
인간의 양심도 계속 무너져 내릴 것이다.
정의도, 허욕도...,
마침내 부질없는 인간의 희망마저도!

Grand Blue (The Great Sea)

- Cherishing the Memory of a Man Who Drowned While Challenging the World Diving Record

Dark blue space, cut off
even from grains of light.
Depth of a bottomless abyss.
A bucket, cast down
to sea floor
from the edge of a deck
swaying at the heart of ocean.

Suspended in a space at standstill,
the sound of a choked heartbeat
counting down the depth of his diving.

Deep blue horizon line, blinding light
like a blessing upon earth,
He fills his eyes with both
As if bidding his last farewell to this world,
filling the whole of his brown chest
with deep breath,
The man casts down his life
without an oxygen mask.

Friendship on surface,
the affection between them
warmer than brotherly love,

그랑 블루(큰 바다)

- 세계잠수기록에 도전하다 익사한 사내의 죽음을 추모하며

빛의 미립자마저 차단된 짙푸른 공간
바없는 심연의 깊이
바다 한가운데 흔들리는 갑판 끝에서
해저海底를 향해 드리워진 두레박
그 정지된 공간에 매달려
잠수의 깊이 카운트 다운하는
숨 막히는 심장 고동소리

짙푸른 수평선, 지상의 축복 같은 눈부신 빛
마지막 이승 작별인사 고하듯
두 눈 가득 담고
깊고 그득한 호흡 구릿빛 가슴에 충만히 채우고
산소마스크도 없이
생명을 투하投下하는 사내

지상에서의 우정
형제애보다 뜨거운 사제 간의 정이
냉엄한 목숨을 건 기록 경쟁으로,
숨이 끊어지는 생사의 갈림길
심해어深海漁 야광등이 저승불 밝히는
아득히 먼 바다 속으로

all sink into the sea faraway,
where the noctilucent lamps of deep-sea fish
glow like lights from the other world,
on the crossroad between life and death
where breathing stops,
Stark competition for which his life is risked.

70m, 80m, 90m, 100m, 110m 113m, 115m 118m 119m
120m...

The pangs of a heart on the verge of crumbling.
Muscle's pain being squeezed,
as if paralyzed.

On the side of boat,
At the point where the ocean has almost halted,
Those who are measuring the time and depth of the dive
Are twitchy, on edge… Fearful…

'Ah, please stop now....
Better come to the surface....'

The man, having lost competition,
refused his return to the surface
was swimming in the deep sea
in absolute loneliness,
peaceful, horizontal
rather than making a breathless, perpendicular descent.

70, 80, 90, 100, 110, 113, 115, 118, 119, 120m...

끊어질 듯한 심장의 고통
마비된 듯 압박해 오는 근육의 통증

뱃전에서, 바다 속 정지된 지점에서
잠수의 깊이와 시간을 재는 자들에게
스멀거리며 곤두서는 동요... 두려움...

'아, 제발 그만
솟구쳐 올라왔으면...'

기록 경쟁에서 지자
끝내 수면水面으로의 귀환 마다하고
숨 막히는 수직의 하강 대신
안온한 수평의 뒤채임으로
심해 그 절대 고독의 허무를
유영하는 사내.

해파리처럼 무상無常 무애無碍 무중력으로
물살 따라 흐름을 맡긴 육신

한 때 그대를 영웅으로 추앙해 준
항시 그대를 넉넉히 품어준 바다
그 넓고 깊은 품안에 안긴
그대의 영혼

His body, like a jellyfish,
entrusted to the currents of sea
with the mutability of the world,
free from all obstacles,
in zero gravity.

Your soul, embraced by
the immense and deep bosom of sea,
that once embracing you as a hero
always embracing you wholeheartedly.

Having poured into the sea
your last handful passion,
having dyed even your stopped heart blue,
you win, at last, your freedom.

---

* Footnote: Divers at the 2012 free diving world cup in the Bahamas probably had
things on their minds other than taking in the beautiful scenery of the picturesque
bay.
The competitors took their lives into their own hands as they dived without air,
with some reaching depths of more than 100 meters.

New Zealand competitor William Trubridge broke a national record as he completed a dive to 121 meters (under constant weight) at the Dean's Blue Hole on
Long Island in the Bahamas. (quoted from Facebook by author)

마지막 한 줌 열정 쏟아 붓고
멎은 심장마저 푸른 빛으로 물들인 그대는
마침내 자유를 얻는다.

---

* 2012년 바하마에서 개최된 'Free Diving World Cup'에서 무산소로 100m 이상 잠수하는 목숨을 건 대결이 벌어졌는데, William Trubridge(뉴질랜드)가 121m를 잠수함으로써 세계기록을 세웠다.(Facebook에서 인용)

The Sea of Fate

- The Summer of 1998, Homeless People in Korea

Flowing to the sea
whether the river wills it or not,
all streams and branching rivers,
currents large and small,
are driven to the sea.

Though salmon and flying fishes
Sometimes swim upstream,
they are but the chosen few.

Fish, mixed in with the current,
swarm, like fate,
into the mouth of the river
and mingled in the vast sea.

Leaving their homes behind,
having lost their beloved families,
the desolation of people
wandering about the boundless sea,
places unfamiliar,
where they can distinguish nothing.

Pushed by surging waves,
caught in a whirlpool of careless currents

운명의 바다

- 1998년, 한국의 홈레스homeless

강이 제 의지와 무관하게
바다로 흘러가듯

모든 시냇물과 샛강
크고 작은 물줄기들이
바다로 내몰리고 있다.

어쩌다 흐름 거스르는
연어, 날치 떼도 있으나
그건 선택받은 소수일 뿐

흐르는 물살에 뒤섞인 물고기들은
숙명처럼 강 하구로 몰려들어
드넓은 바다에서 함께 뒤섞인다.

고향을 등지고
사랑하는 가족마저 잃고
천지사방 분간조차 할 수 없는
낯선 곳
망망대해
떠도는 막막함

되돌아갈 길 잃어버리고
드넓은 바다 위

to spin round and round,
an empty raft that lost its way of return,
shipwrecked in the wide open sea.

In the middle of the sea
no way out.

난파당한 빈 뗏목처럼
넘실대는 파도
무심한 해류의 소용돌이에 휘말려 돌고 있다.

출구 없는 바다 한 가운데서.

Tidal Wave

Likely perhaps every thousand year,
An immense perpendicular departure
From normal course of the horizon,
Bursting forth in great, writhing movement.

Frightened by angry sound of thundershower,
fishing villages, turning deadly pale,
lay flat on the ground.
Even puppies were called into the deep corner
of the fishermen's living room
their wet legs trembling...

Desolate space where
Breakwaters, lighthouses, fishing boats bound somewhere
Lost their shapes, becoming traces of
Oblique lines that poured down wildly.

The fearful dread, as if the Iguasu, Niagara,
Victoria Falls, all together,
were brought high into the sky
flung to the ground.

Are there, in the infinitely mild water,
enormous roots existed

해일

천년에 한 번쯤
일어날 법한,
수평의 일상적 상궤常軌 깨고
엄청난 수직의 일탈逸脫로 솟구치는
저 거대한 용틀임.

노성뇌우怒聲雷雨에 바짝 엎드린
어촌은 푸르죽죽 사색이 되어
강아지새끼마저 안방 깊숙이 불러들인 채
부들부들 젖은 가랑이를 떨고 있을 뿐...

방파제도, 등대도
그 어디쯤 비끌어 매였을 어선들도
거칠게 쏟아지는 사선斜線의 실루엣 흔적으로
지워지고 마는 저 막막한 공간.

이과수, 나이아가라, 빅토리아폭포를
한꺼번에 하늘로 띄워 올려
지상地上에 태질해 대는 듯한
저 가공할 경외로움.

한없이 부드러운 물에도
고래힘줄보다 더 질긴
태양의 흑점보다 더 무서운 폭발력을 지닌

tougher than a whale's muscle,
more terribly explosive
than the spots on the sun?

The explosion of power
beyond comparison, sounds of its tremor,
as if swallowing every sound
on the ground with no exception,
against even the rotation of the earth.

When I awakened to the world,
I glanced at the coast of East Sea
that the sea is not submerged under the sea,
but holds its breath awhile
in the deep abyss,
upon reaching the peak of absolute loneliness,
exhales, at once, its deep, resolute breath.

거대한 뿌리가 존재하고 있는 것일까.
지상의 소리란 소리 죄다 삼키고
지구의 자전自轉마저 거스를 듯
저 광대무비한 힘의 폭발, 진동음.

바다는 바다에 잠겨있는 게 아니라
심연 깊은 곳에서 오랜 숨을 참고 있다가
절대 고독의 정점에서
마침내 어기찬 큰 숨을
한꺼번에 토해낸다는 것을
나는
세상에 눈 뜰 무렵
동해안 바닷가에서 보았다.

Mud Flat

At times a bog
From which there is no escape,
A resurgent organism,
Its windpipes holding,
And filtering all things,
Embracing wounded men.

With its chest as bare as an empty field,
instead of the fullness that embraced the sea,
it hugs grudging starlights,
tossing and turning
during the long night under a full moon.

While leftists and rightists, in turn,
are pushed in and out by the ebb and flow,
a woman shrieked a single cry to her foolish husband
who, aware of the rising tide,
heads to the mud flat:
"Look, look! Come back, quickly!"
Her uvula falls, rolls about somewhere
near the crab holes scattered here and there.

Hanging in a corner of my heart,
the shadow of history awkwardly exits

갯벌

때로는 헤어날 길 없는 수렁이었다가
온갖 것 다 담아 거르는 거대한 숨구멍으로
상처 난 인간 품어 안아주는
부활하는 생명체

바다를 안았던 충만 대신
텅 빈 벌판 같은 맨가슴으로
원망怨望 담긴 별빛 보듬고
보름달 따라 긴 밤 뒤척인다.

좌파, 우파가 밀물 썰물로 밀리고 밀려갈 때
밀물이 차오르는 걸 모르고
개펄로 나서는 어리석은 지아비를 향해
"보소, 보소! 퍼뜩 돌아오소!"
외마디 비명 지르던 아낙의 목젖
숭숭 뚫린 게구멍 어딘가 떨어져 나뒹굴고 있다.

길 없는 길 따라
쫓기듯 어설프게 퇴장하는
역사의 그림자 가슴 한 켠에 드리우고
물기 가득 담은 커다란 눈망울은
그저 무심한 하늘만 우러른다.

기쁨보다는 슬픔이 많았을 세월,

as if being chased, following the roadless road,
and my large eyes, fully moist,
look only upon the uncaring sky.

A time when sadness was
more common than joy,
the original sin of men, still buried,
as splinters jabbed into raw flesh,
in a mud flat of silence as black as charcoal soot.

Yet still dreaming of eternal conciliation
Between heterogeneous beings,
Mother, who connects the naval tethers of life,
How I can miss your bosom?

숯검뎅 같은 검은 침묵의 뻘밭에
생살에 박힌 파편으로
아직도 파묻혀 있을 인간의 원죄.

그래도 이질적 존재와 존재 사이
영원한 화해를 꿈꾸며
생명의 탯줄 잇고 계신 어머니,
당신 품이 그립습니다.

Sea Fog Alarm

The sound of a siren, ringing ardently
from all part, the edge of sea,
to the end of sky,
every corner of earth,
in the tired, early dawn.
A fog alarm siren of sea fog,
which sounds like a boat whistle,
more likely the horn of a boat,
have you ever heard the fog alarm?

The sweet voice guiding ships
lost their way
in the thick fog.

Having drunken heartily
ten glasses of soupy, yeasty makgeolli,
Raw rice wine,
the tasty voice of seaman,
ample with nerves, sings
world wide famous song Santa Lucia, by raising his voice.

To the blind man unable to see an inch,
the voice, leading him kindly,
is surely more valuable than a lamplight.

해무경보

나른한 이른 새벽
바다 끝, 하늘 끝, 땅 끝 구석구석
절절히 울리는 사이렌소리
뱃고동소리만 같은
해무경보海霧警報를 들어 보셨나요?

짙은 안개 속
길 잃은 배를 안내하는
그 구수한 목소리

텁텁한 막걸리
걸쭉하니 열 잔쯤 걸치고
목청 돋워 간만에 싼타루치아 명곡 뽑아 올리는
바다사나이의 뱃심같이
두둑하면서도 넉넉한 음성

한 치 앞도 안 보이는 장님에겐
불빛보다 다정히 이끄는 목소리가 더 소중한 법

왜 똑같은 목소리도
확 트인 넓은 바다
그것도
공기의 밀도가 짙은 안개 속에서
사물과 사물의 구별이 희미해지고
아련한 꿈 속 같은 기억의 켜를 헤집고 들어설 때
더더욱 그리움 같은 목소리로

Why does the same voice
become a voice of longing,
chilling our hearts,
when, on the wide-open seas,
in the thick fog and dense air,
we can no longer tell one object from another,
digging up layers of memories like a dim dream?

Why does the fog alarm, an urgent warning
of danger, of human lives possibly being lost,
to ships, having lost their routes,
of running aground on sunken rocks,
approach us so leisurely?
Why does the siren come to us
as a most affectionate human voice?

Why does it make our whole bodies feel
the pain of restlessness, as if we meet
long-awaited lovers coming along
a bright road of magnolia blossoms?

Perhaps it may bring us
infinitely plaintive love,
vast and wide enough to make
the sky, the sea, the land cry,
yet having to navigate the fog containing fear?

Really, I really don't know...

198   Sea Fog Alarm

가슴 ~~~~려드~~ 걸까요

왜 해무경보는
목숨이 경각을 다툴 수~~~ 있고
항로 잃은 선박이 암초에 ~초될지 모르~
위급함을 알리는 화급한 경~ 인데도
이렇듯 느긋하게 다가서는 것~~까요
사이렌소리가 더없이 정다운 인~의 목소리로
와 닿은 것일까요

목련꽃 벙글어진 환한 꽃길 따라
기다리던 님 오시듯
설렘으로 온몸을 저리게 하는 것일까요

하늘, 바다, 땅을 모두 울릴 만큼 크고 넓은,
그러나 두려움이 함께하는 안개를 헤쳐 나가야 하는
바없이 애잔한 사랑이 함께 깃들여 그런 것일까요

정말 알 수 없는 일입니다.

The Sky and the Sea

Just as we do not search for the road
until we have lost it,
we look for the sea
only after it is lost.

The sea is open window,
our hope and consolation.
An open breast,
our breathing air.

Boundless vault of heaven.
The sky, beginning of this world.

Since genesis,
when water divided to become
the sky and sea,

the sky, yearning for sea,
turns, unpredictably, into rain
to fall to sea,

and the sea, holding the sky underwater,
erases the horizon
with huge, writhing motions like dragons

하늘과 바다

길을 잃고서야 길을 찾듯
바다를 잃고서야
우리는 비로소 바다를 찾는다.

바다는 열린 창
우리의 희망이자 위안
열린 가슴,
숨 쉬는 공기다.

끝없는 궁창
태초의 하늘

물과 물이 나뉘어
하늘과 바다가 된
창세기 천지창조 이래

바다가 그리운 하늘은
무시로 비가 되어 바다로 내리고

하늘이 잠긴 바다는
거대한 용틀임으로 수평선을 지우고
이제 한 몸으로 어우러져 출렁인다.

둥근 우주 속에서

by joining as one, swells.

Just as our heart would be one
longing for our mother
in this round universe....

어머니를 그리는
우리의 마음이 하나이듯...

The Sea Comes as the Sound at Midnight, and Disappears

The sea we yearn for,
turns to rain,
knocks softly on my attic windows
open toward the sky.

Before dawn arrives,
hiding its figure deep in the darkness,
the sea knocks only as a sound,
quiet and low,
caressing our heart.

Ta, ta, ta, ta!
Raindrops approach nearer and nearer.
In no time, the infinite space open to the sky
is filled with the sounds of the sea.

Woo, woo, wong! Woo, woo, wong!
Chua, cha! Chua, cha!
Sounds, unable to become words,
scatter into segments,
voices all the more keenly needed.

Always nearer to the sky than the ground,
Attics, standing on tiptoes,

심야에 소리로 왔다 사라지는 바다

그리운 바다는
비가 되어
가만히
하늘로 열린 다락창문을 두드리고 있다.

새벽이 오기 전
제 모습 어둠 속에 깊이 감춘 채
소리만으로,
가슴 어루만지는 그윽이 낮은 소리

두둑두두두둑
점점 가까이 다가서는 빗방울
어언간 하늘로 열린 무한공간은
바닷소리만으로 그득 찬다.

우우웅우우웅
쏴아쏴아
소리가 말이 되지 못하고
분절음으로 흩어져
외려 더 절실한 음성.

다락은 늘 지상보다
하늘 가까이 발돋움하고 있어
달팽이 더듬이같이 예민하고

Sensitive like the feelers of a snail.
The sound of rain and waves
Intermingled together as
murmurs, near while far.

Like a lover
Disappearing without a trace
After appearing in a dream longed for,
the ground's shadows, high and low,
grow clearer, and spill drops
of salty seawater.

빗소리, 파도소리 함께 뒤엉킨
멀고 가까운 웅얼거림

그리운 이 꿈결에 왔다가
홀연 자취 감추듯 사라지자
선명히 밝아오는
높고 낮은 지상의 그림자
소금기 밴 바닷물을 뚝뚝 흘리고 있다.

The Sea of Avalokitesvara, Buddhist Goddess of Mercy

Hoping to release the word in my heart,
I came to realize
That even this was meaningless.

The sea, surging forth relentlessly
from the steps of sea bottom,
growing deeper towards the middle,
blew away, like foam,
the useless words in my mind
overwhelming me in an instant
with the sound containing infinite silence.

The waves, overflowing into my eyes,
spilled over the emptied wall in my heart,
winding in circles,
coiling around me endlessly.

Nature's ensemble piece,
of heaven and earth, sweeping in
all kinds of high, low voices on the ground,
even the sound from the sky,
to pour them out.

Filling into my heart

관음의 바다

가슴에 담긴 말
토하고파
찾아왔다가
그것마저 부질없는 것임을 알겠더라.

한가운데 나아갈수록
더 깊어지는 해심海心의 계단으로부터
쉬임없이 밀려오는 바다는
부질없는 인간의 언어 포말처럼 날려버리고
한량없는 침묵의 소리로 일순 나를 사로잡아버리더라.

눈동자에 흘러넘친 파도는
비워낸 빈 마음 벽에도 흘러넘쳐
끝 간 데 없이 나를 휘감고 돌더라.

지상의 높고 낮은 목소리
죄다 쓸어 담고
우렁우렁
하늘 소리까지 품어 쏟아내는
저 천상천하 자연의 합주곡

보이는 바다보다
더 큰 바다가 마음에 담기고
비로소 관음觀音의 참뜻에 눈을 뜨겠더라.

invisible sea larger than the one visible,
I was awakened to
the true meaning of Goddess of Mercy.

The horizon lying a slant, as always,
in the shape of praying lying Bucldhist image,
is overlooking waves' tip breaking afar
around its remoted feet having a smile in its lip
as if induging in a dream or asleep...

언제나 그러하듯
수평선은 와선臥하듯 비스듬히 누워
먼발치에서 부서지는 파도 깃을 굽어보며
조으는 듯 꿈꾸는 듯
빙그레 웃음만 머금고 있더라.

Ulleung Island

If you harbor an enigma,
At times drifting like apprehension,
Unable to be solved
By anything on this world.

Go, I recommend you,
to Ulleung Island.

Floating on waves,
Let them carry your body,
that has become as light as a feather.
Go forward without pause
Over, and again over, the horizon.

Cliffs, stepping on blue waves,
nimbly soar upward,
and the crying of sea swallows,
those pecking at the edge of the sky,
between this world and the next,
against winds like knifeblades,
rush towards you.

You will see, as if in a dream,
The familiar face of a brother,

울릉도

때로는
시름처럼
떠도는,
이 세상 무엇으로도
풀 길 없는
화두話頭 하나
간직하고 있거든

그대
울릉도로 가게나.

두둥실
파도 깃에
새털처럼 가벼워진 몸을 싣고
수평선 굽이굽이
넘고 또 넘어
쉬임없이 짓쳐 가노라면

푸른 물결 자락 즈려 밟고
가뿐히 솟구친 벼랑
칼날 같은 바람 거스르며
이승과 저승 오가듯
하늘 끝 쪼아대는
바다제비들 울음소리

Forgotten like oblivion itself,
One name, coming back,
Brilliantly resurrected in this world.

Glasses of soju, distilled liquor,
Drinking before lamps
of a squid fishing boat.
Ah!
At Dodong Port,
illuminated by full moon,
revealing even the core
of original sin,
I swallow, until dawn, shame
that I have no way of hiding,

I cannot clarify
When, and from where
Life's knots began to tangle,
How I arrived here,
My repentances repeated…

The cup of shame can never be filled,
though it swallows the sea.
The substance of original sin
as clear as the transparent, like thin veins
of a squid's raw body.

If you wish to recover new life,

저 먼저 달려오고
망각인양
오래도록 잊고 산
낯익은 형제의 얼굴로
한 아름
가슴 안겨오는
이승에서의 눈부신 환생還生
꿈결엔 듯 보게 될 걸세.

오징어잡이배 등불 마주하고
기울이는 소주잔,
아,
원죄의 속살까지
화안히 비치는
도동항 보름달빛 아래
신새별 다하도록
감출 길 없는 부끄러움 삼키며

되짚어도 보나
언제 어디서부터 얽혀
예까지 와 닿았는지
도무지 가늠할 길 없는
삶의 매듭, 거듭된 참회...

부끄럼의 잔은
저 바다를 들이켜도 다함 없고
원죄의 실체는
회 친 오징어 투명한 실핏줄마냥 선명하다.

I dare to tell you,
go to Ulleung Island.

The shapes of imposing rocks,
like those of myth, heighten their strength
toward the sky
Cradled in the island's ample bosom,
prepared for a thousand years hence,
get a son, healthy and strong.

Will you dredge up
Fresh cry, strong enough
to shake the world vehemently?

그대
새로웁게 삶을 시작하려거든
울릉도로 가게나.

신화神話 속엔 듯싶은 우람한 바위들의 형상
하늘 향해 힘겨룸하는,
천년쯤 후를 위해
예비해 둔
그 넉넉한 품속에 안겨
실하고 튼튼한
옥동자 하나 얻어 보게나.

온 세상
쩌렁쩌렁
울리고도 남을
싱싱한 울음소리
건져 올려 보게나.

Wave

Always full and overflowing.

Charming abundance
of a woman's bobbing breast.
Abundant chest pacifying
your unfulfilled dream.

The root of life,
tougher than a whale's sinew.
Diving without weariness
Your fighting spirit, today as before,
Darts off like a thousand riding horses,
Mane raised,
running across a wild field.

The blue wind, rising breathlessly
at the end of mane,
Pieces of life breaking
along with your breath.

Tolerance gathering all.
Paradox of the ego refusing the whole.
Endless dream embraces all of them
and sinks in the abyss of the other world.

파도

늘상 차고 넘친다.

출렁이는 여인의 유방
그 황홀한 풍요로움.
그대 못다 이룬 꿈
위무慰撫하는 드넓은 가슴.

고래힘줄보다 질긴
목숨의 뿌리
지침 없는 자맥질
그대 투혼은
오늘도 거친 벌판 치닫는
말갈기 세우며
천군만마千軍萬馬로 내달린다.

갈기 끝
숨차게 일어서는 푸른 바람,
더불어 깨어지는 생명生命의 조각들.

모든 것을 거두는 관용
일체를 거부하는 에고의 역설逆說
함께 보듬고
구천심연九泉深淵 함몰하는
다함 없는 꿈,

Stepping on the edge of a knife
and bumping against a precipice,
these, at last, turn into a handful of foam,
and disappear...

Still today in the field of one's dreams,
Coarse and unclutivatable,
The seed of life, carried on one's back and discarded,
lies buried at sea
in an empty marsh covered with sand.

칼끝 밟고 단애에 부딪쳐
끝내
한 줌 포말로 사라지고 마는 것을...

오늘도
일구지 못한 성긴 꿈의 텃밭에
등짐 져 버린 생명의 씨앗,
빈 모래펄에 수장手葬된다.

The Flock of Seagulls Flying Over Open Sea of Daepo Port

Morning on Korean Peninsula
first arrives on the East Sea,
particularly, to Daepo Port
between Yangyang and Sokcho city.

At dawn, as if blessing the fishing boats
just before leaving port,
a flock of seagulls,
of thousands or tens of thousands,
hovers around the masts in disorder.

Carrying on each feather shaken off
The brightest, purest sunlight,
Blue currents are kicked up vigorously.

Each mingles with one another to
dance in groups, and then,
in an instant, they soar up together,
a silvery fish as fresh as a bundle of light
caught on each beak.

The strength of their solemn gestures,
so dazzling that the sun
would rather shut its eyes.

대포 앞바다를 나는 갈매기떼

한반도의 아침은
동해바다 하고도,
양양과 속초 사이
대포 앞바다에서 먼저 온다.

새벽녘 출항을 앞둔 고깃배
축복이나 하듯
어지럽게 마스트 주면 오가는
수천수만 마리 갈매기떼
떨치는 깃털마다에
가장 눈부시고 순결한
햇살 무리 실어
힘차게 푸른 물살을 차고 든다.

그리곤 저마다 어우러져
군무를 추다가 일순,
빛의 다발 같은 싱싱한
은빛 고기 입에 물고
일제히 박차 오른다.

그 장엄한 몸짓들의 강렬함
해마저 눈부셔 도리어 눈을 감고
갈매기들은
이제 스스로가 빛의 발광체가 되어

The seagulls have become luminous bodies
flying over the vast sea,
again brightens the day
from land to the sea.

Towards dawn
their gestures, start very first before others
to fight for survival
are so pure and dazzlingly beautiful,
more than anything else in the world.

I realized it in front of the open sea
of Daepo Port.

저 너른 바다를 날며
육지에서 바다로 다시 날을 밝힌다.

해 돋을 무렵
가장 먼저 생존의 투쟁을 시작하는
그들의 몸짓이야말로
이 세상 그 어느 것보다
순결하고 눈부시도록 아름답다는 걸

나는 대포 앞바다에서 보았다.

제4부 이국시 / 한국시

Part four *Exotic Poems / Korean Poems*

Lorelei

The wind does not exist only as itself,
and when a hill cannot stand alone as a hill,
our yearning song turns into a river water
hiding crying in its depth,
and releases little by little.

Burning desire, unfulfilled on the ground,
Soar high into the sky,
Loosening their disheveled hair as they please,
creeping into disheveled leaves, of tree stood on top of
Lorelei hill
and poking hard at tender, crying hearts,
to awaken each of them.

Lorelei hill cannot be aware of to those
who have never encounter the soul of the wailing wind.
Greeting the wind crossing a barren field,
a dancer performs gypsy dance.
At the peak of her dance, a man pulls her to his chest
grabbing her breast, as if kneading,
with hands as tough as a plough,
drags scream from her mouth,
but even that is snatched
by the wind's snare, is

로렐라이

바람이 바람만으로 존재하지 않고
언덕이 언덕으로 홀로 서 있지 못할 때
우리들의 노래는 속울음 깊은 강물 되어
시나브로 풀린다.

지상에서 이룰 수 없어 하늘 향해 솟구친 염원들,
헝클어진 머리칼 한껏 풀어헤치고
무심한 나뭇잎 잎새에까지 파고들어
그 여린 속살울음 속속들이 들쑤셔 깨우고 있다.

울부짖는 바람의 넋이 되어보지 못한 자는
로렐라이 언덕을 알지 못한다.
거친 벌판 가로질러 오는 바람 맞이하며
짐시 춤을 추는 무희舞姬,
춤의 절정에서 여인을 가슴팍까지 끌어들인 사내는
쟁기같이 억센 손으로 반죽하듯
무희의 젖가슴을 움켜쥐며
외마디 비명 이끌어내나
그마저 바람의 덫에 채여 휑한 골짝으로
흩어져 부서지고 만다.

해 저물자 물오리 떼 이따금 추억의 잔상殘像

scattered and smashed in a hollow valley.

The shores of Rhine where,
under the setting sun, a flock of wild ducks
at times search for the remnants of memories.
The long shadow of a freighter laden iron ore,
having stopped its weary voyage.
An imposing, shabby castle of ghost
that holds the trace of people who have left,
no longer belonging to this world,
along with flags that were once glorious,
drops anchor deep into the dark silence of time,
the voices from this world and the world beyond
joined to form a shallow stream.

Having lighted two or three short candles
on a stone step,
flickering as if dancing to the tender night breeze,
One German young woman, tuning guitar strings,
sends softly into the air
folk melodies like delicate, white papers
burned to the god.

Her longing voice
can be heard only to those possessing a quiet,
serene leisure, who can find starlight hidden in the
bright stars.
to count those hidden.

뒤척이는 라인강변,
지친 항해 멈춘 철광석 실은 화물선 긴 그림자
이미 이 세상이 아닌
저 세상 사람들의 혼적 담아내고 있는
저 우람하고 남루한 유령의 성城,
한 때는 영광이었을 깃발과 함께
캄캄한 시간의 정적 깊숙이 닻을 내리고
이승과 저승의 목소리 한데 어우러져 여울진다.

여린 밤바람에 춤추듯 어른거리는
키 낮은 촛불 두엇 돌계단에 뉘어놓고
기타줄 조율하며
허공에 나지막이 띄우는 소지燒紙 같은
여인의 노랫가락
찬연한 별빛 가리면서 숨은 별빛 헤아리는
고즈넉한 여유를 가진 자에게만 들리는
그대 그리운 목소리.

로렐라이언덕은
너무나 아스라해 쉽게 찾을 수 없다.

넘실대는 구릉과 구릉 사이 아스라이 파묻혀
성과 마을, 둔덕, 포도밭과 옥수수, 밀밭 길 따라
이제는 호텔이 되어버린 12세기 수도원
때로는 너무나 평화롭게 잠든 공동묘지를 지나

The hill of Lorelei is too hazy
to be easily found.

Buried between rolling hills,
down a road past
a castle and village, knolls, vineyards
and fields of corn and wheat,
a monastery of the 12th century, now a hotel,
a public cemetery, its tenants sound asleep
perhaps too peacefully.
At last, at the edge of a delta
Where poplar trees, raised carelessly,
line in a single file
along the meandering river hides its naked body,
Lorelei crosses its plump legs
shyly, with the body of a mature woman,
melts into the landscape.

Lorelei is hidden
like a lover in a heartrending landscape,
Invisible to those who search for it,
And once seen, appears to recede,
like our tragic course in life
in which lovers, living side by side,
die without being united.

Still today, resurrected as the wind,
she wanders about the countless, unknown hills, singing

굽이치는 강물이 벌거벗은 몸 가리며
아무렇게나 키운 포플러가 일렬종대로
늘어서 있는 삼각주 끝
로렐라이는 수줍은 듯 풍만한 다리를 포개고
성숙한 여인의 몸매로 풍경 속에 녹아들어 있다.

찾는 자에게는 보이지 않고
보이는 순간 아득히 멀어져 가는
애달픈 풍경 속 그리운 연인처럼,
혹은 바로 곁에 있으나 끝내 짝이 되지 못하고
이승을 마감해야 하는
비극적인 우리네 인생사처럼
로렐라이는 그렇게 숨어있다.

바람으로 부활한 그녀는
오늘도 이름 모를 무수한 언덕을 떠돌며
바람의 높이만큼
옥타브 높여 노래하고 있다.
뼈저린 가난과 이별의 고통에 목놓아 울어본 자에게만
다가와 안기는 로렐라이.
절망적이고도 황홀한 사랑.

인생의 정점에서 한여름밤 꿈처럼 흘러가 버린
젊음과 이상理想의 부질없음을 깨닫고
모든 것을 체념했을 때

in an octave as high as the harsh wandering wind.
Approaching only those who have wept with abandon
from the pain of poverty and agony of parting,
Lorelei throws herself for those who suffered desperate
yet entrancing love.

From the peak of life, short-lived youth
and ideals were realized momentarily,
having flowed by like a summer night's dream,
and when all abandoned,
All of a sudden, you can hear a voice
from the sky draws near,
rushing barefoot from this and that valley,
mingling with the river water to shake
and awaken sleeping soul.

Having heard your so lovely seductive voice,
Oh! I feel ecstasy, so happy Today...

홀연 다가서는 하늘의 소리,
이 골짝 저 골짝 맨발로 내달리며
강물에 뒤섞여 잠자는 영혼靈魂 흔들어 깨우는
고혹적인 그대 목소리를 듣는
오늘 하루 나는 행복하다.

Ganges River

So wide, so deep.
Does the world you have been dreaming of
open its eyes, approaching
like a new day breaking
from the remote end of the other world?

When the pains of a body, hungry and thirsty end,
death is embracing you
under the scorching heat of the sun,
for that very reason,
your dream of rebirth
is unable to be abandoned.

Sullying even the road to the other world,
insects burrow into corpses
with swarming worms.
The estuary of the Ganges river
where dead bodies float by
like rotten tree trunks.

When will the Ganges river also surge with
the green waves of the Lotus Lake, Imdangsoo*

갠지스강

넓고 깊어
아득한 저 세상 끝에서
새날이 밝아오듯
그대 꿈꾸던 세상
눈떠 오는가.

굶주리고 기갈 든 육신의 고통
다하고
뜨거운 불볕 아래
맞이한 죽음,
그러기에 더욱 버릴 수 없는
환생에의 꿈.

저승길마저 어지럽히며
파고드는 곤충
우글거리는 뭇 벌레떼
썩은 나무등걸 같은 시신
둥둥 떠다니는
갠지스강 하구.

언제쯤
갠지스강에도
죽음이

where death blossoms into lotus flowers
brilliantly smiling?

---

* Lotus Lake, Imdangsoo ;

Legendary imaginary lake located Yellow Sea near Hwanghae province, North Korea.
That place is well known to Koreans as holy dedicated place in old days.
There is legend like this.

'The sailors donated young pretty woman to Dragon King in compensation of
abundant fishing & safe journey at Imdangsoo.

Pretty young woman named Simchung sacrified herself to open eyes for her blind
old father. She was drown but the Dragon King saved her life because Dragon
King was deeply impressed by her faithfulness to her poor father in illness.

The story close happy ending; Blind poor father opened his eyes under the mercy
of King dragon in the sea while Simchung got married with King Dragon.'

(by author)

환한 연꽃으로 피어오르는

임당수 푸른 물 넘실거릴까.

---

* 임당수 :

  북한 황해도 인근 황해바다에 위치한 상상 속의 바다호수로서 예전부터 성스러운 것을
바치는 장소로 알려져 있다.

  뱃사람들이 임당수를 무사히 항해하고 물고기를 많이 잡게 해 달라고 용왕에게 젊고 예쁜
여인을 바치는 풍습이 있었다.

  예쁜 젊은 처녀인 심청은 눈 먼 늙은 아버지의 눈을 뜨게 해 달라고 자신을 바쳤다.

  심청은 물에 빠져 죽게 되었으나 병든 아버지를 구하려는 효심에 감동한 용왕이 자비를
베풀어 심청을 살려주었을 뿐 아니라 그녀를 아내로 맞이하고 심청아버지 눈을 뜨게 해 준
다는 해피엔딩으로 이야기가 끝난다.

Rembrant, Painter of Shadow

The late afternoon when I met you
in early Autumn,
I was being harassed
by the cold, bleak raindrop
scattering from the cloudy sky
of Amsterdam, turned into
thick shadow of dispair gathering
on potatoes of the soily basket
painted by Van Gogh.

No! No! No!

To embrace the thread of life,
the last shadow of Jesus dragged to Golgotha Hill
looking over his shoulder
at Peter, who had rejected him thrice
trembling in fear,
at early dawn the rooster crowed.

The silent words cast by the brush,
as sharp as a scalpel,
scooped out the shameful
conscience of humankind.

그림자 화가 렘브란트

그대를 만난 초가을 늦은 오후,
암스테르담 흐린 하늘에서 흩뿌리는
춥고 음산한 빗방울이
반 고흐가 빚어낸
흙 묻은 바구니 속 감자에 고여 있는
짙은 절망의 그늘이 되어
내내 나를 괴롭혔다.

아니오, 아니오, 아니오,

실낱같은 생의 끈 부둥켜 안으려 두려움에 떨며
자신을 세 번 부인하는 베드로를
설핏 뒤돌아보며
새벽닭 우는 이른 새벽,
골고다 언덕으로 끌려가는
예수의 마지막 그림자.

인류의 부끄러운 양심을 도려내는
저 집도執刀날 같은 붓의 묵언默言.

Notre Dame Cathedral in a Picture

Under the mossy Mirabeau and Pont Neuf Bridge
as if catching the passage of time,
Flows the Seine, and beyond that,
Notre Dame Cathedral.

On a bridge, well-ordered gas lamps are lit,
a woman, raising herself to the height of the gaslight,
is climbing slowly the stone steps,
and a cruise ship is anchored
as if waiting for someone.

The Paris in my memory from twelve years ago,
was capricious, fickle.
within one day in late October,
the sky was clear, then cloudy,
then sleet rained down, followed by fierce wind.

Buried in work as if meditating in the desert
For two whole years,
I was at last freed and could have my fill,
the feeling of flying to heaven
while feasting on culture and civilization.
Luxurious Versailles Palace,
Spectacular Louvre museum,

그림 속의 노트르담사원

세월의 흐름 잡힐 듯 다가서는
이끼 낀 미라보 혹은 퐁네프다리,
그 밑을 흐르는 세느강 너머
노트르담사원은 서 있다.

다리 위 정연히 켜진 가스등,
가스등 높이만큼 키를 돋운
여인이 천천히 돌계단을 오르고 있고
유람선 한 척 언제부턴 듯
누군가를 기다리듯 정박해 있다.

12년 세월 거슬러
회상回想 속의 파리는 변덕스러웠다.
10월 하순 하늘은 하루 동안에도
개었다, 흐렸다, 진눈깨비가 내렸다가
매운바람이 불곤 했다.

2년 꼬박 사막에서 면벽面壁하듯
일에 파묻혀 지내다가
천국으로 날아가듯
문화와 문명의 성찬 만끽하며
베르사유궁전의 호사스러움,
루브르박물관의 장관
개선문 휘황한 샹젤리제 거리

Champs Elysees street so brilliant,
with the Arc of Triumph,
the ancient capital, viewed from Eiffel Tower,
looking more than beautiful.

Yet the only thing left in my heart was
the land near the airport, weedy,
abandoned and uncultivated,
together with the unfettered freedom of cafes,
open spaces harmonized with nature
where our imagination flourishes as it pleases.

The sturdy fortress, looking ever more dignified
From between the shades of trees along the Seine,
reveals itself though hidden, melting
into the landscape regardless of distance.
The Notre Dame Cathedral, so graceful
in my memory, legend
telling a sad love float upward
like a hunchback, unsightly but beautiful.

Today, sitting unnamed café at the foot of Bukhan Mountain,
It approaches me, filling the space of waiting,
by forming single picture
Hanging on a dimly lit wall.

Ah! This fresh longing
that pierces the distance of twelve years in a flash,
like a burning scar, never be erased!

에펠탑에서 굽어본 고도古都는 더없이 아름다웠으나

정작 가슴에 남는 것은
가꾸지 않고 버려둔 공항 변 잡풀 우거진 풍경
자연과 어우러져 열린 공간으로
한껏 상상력을 키워주는
화사한 카페의 분방한 자유스러움.

세느강 변 나무그늘 사이로
볼수록 기품있고
원근 가림없이 풍경에 녹아들어
감춘 듯 드러나는 견고한 성채
애절한 사랑의 전설이 때로는
추하나 아름다운 곱사등으로 솟아오르는
기억 속 수려한 노트르담사원.

오늘 북한산 기슭 이름 없는 카페
조명 흐린 벽면에 걸린 한 폭의 그림으로
기다림의 공간 메우며 다가온다.

아,
12년 세월 단숨에 꿰뚫고
화인火印처럼 지워지지 않는 선연한 그리움.

Everything is Beautiful on the Street of Ginza, Tokyo*

Wandering starlights are gathered together
in Ginza by a vague longing.

Women's curiosity is beautiful,
who glance furtively
at the splendid clothes in shop windows,
and Salary men's generous laughing
expressions relaxed, arms around each other's shoulders,
is enough to fill the street.

At Ginza's entrance, the bugle of avant-garde art
is blown by sounds of computer music,
raising up pieces of fluttering white cloth
that look like ghost.
In the midst of refined street,
A snack cart vendor, tin chimney sprouted high,
Marches onward, without pause, singing loudly
Through a bashed-in bugle.

Having peeped into this street and that,
of neon signs, flashy yet never splendid,
dim fantasies, filtered through prisms of
seven colors of the rainbow, harmonized
tenderly with one another in similar colors and charm,
I enter a cafe. There, the body of a piano

긴자에서는 모두가 아름답다*

긴자에는 떠도는 별빛들이
아련한 그리움으로 한데 모여 있다.

쇼윈도우 화려한 의상을 훔쳐보는
여인의 호기심이 아름답고
풀린 표정으로 어깨동무한
샐러리맨들의 관대한 웃음만으로도
거리는 흘러넘친다.

긴자 입구에는 유령 같은 허연 헝겊
들쑤셔 올리는 컴퓨터음악이
전위예술의 나팔을 울리고
한껏 세련된 거리 한복판을
양철 굴뚝 뽑아 올린 포장마차 장수가
찌그러진 나팔로 고성방가, 내처 행진한다.

현란하나 결코 화려하지 않은 네온,
일곱 무지개빛 프리즘에 여과된
아슴프레한 환상들이 엇비슷한 때깔로
정다운 조화 이루는
이 골목 저 골목 기웃거리다가
카페에 들어서면
피아노 몸체가 허공에 떠올라
구름무늬 유리창에 걸려 있는 파격이

Was afloat in the air and hanging on a window
of cloud patterns, its irregularity
looking rather natural.
The posterior view of a lame, old man
collecting wastepaper looking dearer to me
Than those drunk and sauntering men.

In Ginza, flower shops, toy shops with teddy bears,
galleries, bars serving skewered food, pop saloons
and tea houses line the streets
like the toes of padded socks.

Above all, the coquettish charms of women
wearing Kimono clothes are peerless,
emptying men's pockets.

Ginza, the place of dreams, music and women,
is beautiful.

Having filled our empty pockets
with floating starlights, we prepare
to start a journey to distant space...

Everything is beautiful in Ginza,
even our acute loneliness,
inevitably exposed, staggering.

---

* This poem was transformed to Poetical Drama in the event of 'Simsang Seashore
Poet School' annually organized by Simsang magazine and broadcasted by KBS
radio midnight music programme 'To those who miss Night' in 1985.

자연스럽고
휴지를 주워담는 절름발이 노인의 뒷모습,
술 취해 어정거리는 남정네보다 더 정겹다.

긴자에는 꽃집, 곰인형 아가집, 화방,
꼬치구이집, 팝살롱, 찻집이
버선코 늘어놓듯 고만고만 즐비하고
무엇보다 남자 주머니 훑어 내려는
기모노여인의 간드러진 애교가 일품이다.

꿈과 음악, 여인이 있는
긴자는 아름답다.

빈 주머니 하나 가득
떠다니는 별빛들로 채운 우리들은
먼 우주로 떠날 채비를 차리고...

긴자에서는 모두가 아름답다.
어쩔 수 없이 드러나 비틀거리는
우리의 절실한 고독조차도.

---

* 이 시는 1985년 시전문지 〈심상〉이 주관한 해변시인학교에서 시극(詩劇)으로 무대에 올
  려져 KBS Radio 심야음악프로그램 〈밤을 잊은 그대에게〉를 통해 전국에 방영되었다.

The Bridge that Joins Eternity

- The Bridge of Madison County, USA

Specks of cloud like longing,
appearing and disappearing on a whim
with fresh wind currents
in the sky, high and blue...

Leaves flutter as whisper of souls
having cast off skins of their bodies,
those remained only a moment
on the corner of a vast continent...

The roof of Roseman Bridge,
still retaining Indian decoration,
seems to have endured silently
encarved harsh passage of time.
Covered by the roof, comfortable feeling in the shadow,
The uneasy feeling as if someone may approach
from the shadow, holding out their hand,

The short-lived encounter in this world
that fortunately joins eternity to eternity,
will ripple in your heart
memories of beautiful, sorrowful love
like a song of overflowing joy
soaring endlessly into the clear sky.

영원을 잇는 다리
- 메디슨 카운티의 다리

높푸른 하늘,
싱그런 바람자락 따라
무시로 피었다 스러지는
그리움 같은 구름송이들...

거대한 대륙 한 켠,
잠시 머물다 가는 육신의 허물
벗어버리고
영혼의 속삭임으로 나부끼는 잎새들...

더러는 거친 세월
묵묵히 견뎌 왔음직한
인디언장식 남아있는 로즈먼다리의 지붕
지붕 덮인 그늘의 안온함,
그 그늘 속에서 누군가 손을 내밀고
다가올 듯한 설렘으로

짧은 이승의 인연이
영원을 잇는 자연自然으로,
싱그런 하늘
끝없이 피어오르는
벅찬 환희의 노래처럼
그대 가슴에 물결쳐 올
아름답고 슬픈 사랑의 추억

The love in Madison County
to which I wish to offer
an armful of wild flowers,
unnamed, of all kinds, blossoming
and scattered around me.

Though they are gone and no more,
the Roseman Bridge still remains.

As your love
that joins eternity...

이름 없이 흩어져 피어난 주변의 모든 풀꽃
한 아름 모두어 경건히 바치고 싶은
메디슨 카운티에서의 사랑

그들은 가고 없어도
로즈먼다리는 남아 있다.

영원을 잇는
그대의 사랑으로....

Love Like that of Heine

Though he won the duel
On which he risked his life,
The poor man lost his lover
To his wounded rival.

The poet who grew old,
living alone in loneliness,
on a corner of the park
where he takes his walk, found
a lost country girl, weeping
on a lonely bench.
Hearing her sad story,
He took care of her
At his lodging.

In a flash, the girl transformed
into a dazzlingly beautiful woman.
Heine, a gray-haired, old man, burned
with a wild, passionate love for her.

The anguishing poet left behind for her
the poem 'Du bist wie eine Blume'
(You remain beautiful as a flower)
and resolutely departed.

하이네 같은 사랑

목숨 건 결투에서는 이겼으나
연인은 부상당한 연적戀敵의 품에 빼앗긴
불쌍한 사내.

쓸쓸히 독신으로 늙어가던
시인이 산책하던 공원 한 구석
호젓한 벤치,
길 잃고 훌쩍이는 시골처녀 딱한 사연 듣고
하숙집으로 데려가 돌보아주었네.

잠깐 사이 눈부시도록 아름다운 숙녀로 변신한 소녀
희끗한 귀밑머리 하이네는 주체 못할 연정에 가슴 태웠네.

고뇌하던 시인은
'Du bist wie eine Blume' (너는 한 송이 꽃과도 같이)
시 한 편을 그녀에게 남기고 홀연히 떠나버렸네.

긴긴 세월이 흐른 지금,
이름 없는 코리아의 시인은 여전히 꿈꾸고 있다네.

너무나 맑고 애틋해

Now, a long, long time has flowed,
an unknown poet in Korea still dreams

Of the German poet's love,
So pure and ardent,
As foolish as inevitable parting
With a broken heart.

끝내 가슴 저미며 헤어질 수밖에 없는

그런 바보 같은 독일 시인의 사랑을...

After Being Embraced by Mountain*

The mountain looking at from afar
was merely a piece of landscape.

However, embraced by the mountain
and having walked the path
along which it exhales,
the mountain opens for the first time
the door of its silence
and leaps into me, familiar
as if an old acquaintance of mine,

like the color of maple leaves
soaking into hemp clothes.

Mountain does not seek us out.

It just stands in its place,
but induces our steps
into its large, rich bosom,
and, at last, embraces tightly
even our ultimate death.

Since entering the mountain
and feeling its metaphor with my whole body,

산의 품에 든 후*

거리를 두고 바라보는 산山은
한낱 풍경으로 머물 뿐이지만

山의 품에 들어
山이 내쉬는 숨길 따라
산길을 걷고 나면
비로소 山은 스스로의 침묵을 열어
오랜 구면의 친구인양 허물없이
내 속에 스며든다.

단풍잎이 삼베옷에 물들듯 그렇게.

山은 결코 우리를 찾아 나서지 않는다.

그는 늘상 그 자리에 섰을 뿐이나
언제나 크고 넉넉한 품안으로
우리의 발길 이끌어 들이고
마침내는
우리의 죽음까지 깊이 포옹한다.

山에 들어
山의 은유를 온몸으로 느낀 후
山은 이제 스쳐가는 풍경이 아니라
내 속에 들어와 우뚝 선

Mountain was no longer a landscape passing by,
but an immovable ideology
that, entering me, stood tall firmly.

Shining speculation, shaking
as if visible in silence,
the unrelenting, clear sound of water
touching around the edge of my heart.

A tree, gentle but virile, took root
on a corner of mountainside
A syllable of a mountain bird's song
came down to dwell on the branch,
the sky is nearer
to my forehead.

---

* Seoul Metropolitan published this poem on the screen door of Gangnam Express
Bus Terminal, 3rd Metro line in Seoul

움직일 수 없는 사상思想이 되었다.

침묵 속 보일 듯 흔들리는 빛나는 사유,
가슴 언저리 끊임없이 청량한 물소리.

산비탈 한 켠에 뿌리내린
온유하나 강건한 나무 한 그루,
산새 울음소리 한 소절
내려와 깔리고
하늘은 이마에 한결 가까워 있다.

---

* 이 시는 서울특별시 지하철 3호선 강남고속버스터미널역 screen door에 실려 있음.

Tree

A tree knows how to discard
when the time comes.

Unable to throw away even a hair,
man brings it to his coffin,
but a tree does not leave
even traces of its shadow,
discarding even more, hurriedly,
when those around are not watching.

Standing by your side,
the wind cries peculiarly loudly.
Discarding, and again discarding yourself,
by following the wind.

you do not resist
until the last of your skin is cast off.

The cleverness to protect oneself
by discarding, to prepare more.
The wisdom to ready oneself
to endure the long winter.

When you erase even the traces

나무

나무는 때가 되면 버릴 줄 안다.

인간은 터럭 하나 버리지 못하고
관棺속까지 지니고 가지만
나무는 주위의 눈길이 머물지 않을 때
서둘러
더 많은 것을 버리면서
그림자의 흔적마저 남기지 않는다.

네 곁에 서면
유별나게 크게 우는 바람.
바람 따라 저를 버리고 또 버리고
마지막 한 점 허물을 벗을 때까지
조금도 저항하지 않는다.

버림으로써 저 스스로를 지키는,
더 많은 것을 예비하는 총명.
긴 겨울의 인고를 준비하는 지혜.

하늘을 가린 한 줌의 그늘마저
그 흔적을 지울 때
마침내 너는 온전한 맨 눈과
천둥벌거숭이 맨 가슴으로
지아비의 하늘같은

of the handful of shade that covered the sky,
you finally embrace the sky,
the same as that of your husband,
with your whole, bare eyes
and pure naked chest.

At last, the sky and tree become one...

그 하늘을 껴안는다.

그리하여... 하늘과 나무는 하나가 된다.

Door

The door is close by,
though it seems open to all directions,
it does not reveal itself easily.

The door is stubborn.
Though it seems to open
when the bar across it leans backwards,
the bar is as strong as cast iron,
not squeaking in the slightest.

Concrete walls, the giant buildings of cities
can be destroyed or built
by a stick of dynamite or the power of gold,
but a door is tough.

Those who have the mineral searchlight eyes,
glittering in the darkness, will never know.
They can never measure the depth of door.

Oh, conquerors who returned as triumphant general
after conquering this land,
having made all the sky
and sea cry, will never recognize.

문

문은 지척에 있고
천지사방 열려 있는 듯 보이나
쉽사리 스스로를 드러내지 않는다.

문은 완강하다.
결지른 빗장 젖히면
열릴 듯하나
빗장은 삐꺽 소리조차 내지 않고
무쇠처럼 굳건하다.

다이너마이트 하나로
혹은 황금의 위세로
콘크리트 벽,
거대한 도시의 빌딩은
단숨에 무너뜨리거나 지을 수 있지만
문은 결코 만만치 않다.

어둠 속 번득이는 서치라이트의
광물성 눈을 가진 자들은
알지 못한다.
문의 깊이를 넘보지 못한다.

온 하늘, 온 바다
다 울리고 마침내 이 땅을 정복하고

You may open
The door by force, but even then,
The door is not truly open.

Doors may seem to be scattered every where,
but will never open themselves.

The door only opens itself
for freedom obtained by spilled blood,
or for the truthful person
who is singularly loved.

돌아온 자들이여,
그대들은 알지 못한다.
설령 그대들이 폭력으로 문을 열어젖혔다 할지라도
그 문은 결코 열린 것이 아니다.

문은 천지사방 널려 있어 보이나
문은 스스로를 열어 주는 법이 없다.

문은 저 스스로를 열 따름이다.
피 흘려 얻은 자유, 혹은
사랑하는 오직 한 사람만의 진실을 위해.

If I Could Flow Transparently Like Water...

If I erased all thought,
forgot even the sea in which my body is steeped,

let an inflated air bladder
and open gills,

in the deep sea of absolute silence,
where only plankton swims hazily
in between swaying seaweed,

would my body's rings, scales
that, like tree, grow
differently in summer and winter,
also stop its growth?

If I cast off even these scales
and entrust my raw flesh,
only with the most tender flesh,
surrender to a quiet current,
then, at last, could I also become
the flowing water?

물과 같이 투명하게 흐를 수 있다면...

일렁이는 해초 사이
플랑크톤만이 희뿌옇게 헤엄치는
절대적막 심해深海 속에

부레만 부풀린 채
아가미만 열어놓고

온갖 생각 다 지우고
몸 담근 바다마저 잊는다면

나무와 같이
여름 겨울 다르게 자란다는
내 몸의 나이테비늘도
그 성장을 멈출까

그 비늘마저 벗고
맨살로
연하디 연한 살만으로
고요한 흐름에 맡긴다면
나도 마침내
흐르는 물살이 될 수 있을까.

The Place to Dry Alaska Pollacks

Water drops fall one by one.

Sins that stained their organs,
their futile relations in this world,
discarded on the sand pit
without a speck left behind.

Wide open mouths...
Glaring eyes,
a procession of eyes...

If dead bodies, like this, were gathered,
and neatly hung out to dry,
would it not be an absurd comedy?

The solemn military parade
of Alaska pollacks,
noses pierced
by the horizon of East Sea.

Bathed in the withering winter sun,
their bodies melt and freeze, repeatedly,
as if warming themselves beside a dying bonfire.
They discard themselves completely

황태 덕장

뚝뚝 떨어져 내린다.

오장육부 절은 죄
부질없는 이승에서의 인연
한 점 남김없이 모래판에 부린다.

딱 벌어진 아가리...
부릅뜬 눈, 눈들의 행렬.

이렇듯 주검도 한꺼번에 모아 가지런히 널어놓으면
우스꽝스러운 희극을 연출하는 것일까.

동해바다 수평선에
코 꿴 황태들의 장엄한 열병식.

꺼져가는 화톳불 곁불 쬐듯
아쉬운 겨울해로
얼어 박힌 살 풀었다, 녹였다 하며
더 버릴 것 없을 때까지
누렇게 뜬 살이 뼈다귀를 바를 마지막 순간까지
철저히 너를 버린다.

캄캄한 어둠 속
관 속에서 온 몸의 물 썩어 내리는

until nothing more is left to discard,
at the moment when their flesh,
separating from bones, turns yellow.

How blessed is their death,
more than that of men
whose bodies decay in coffins
of total darkness!

The sun and moon,
moonlight and starlight,
day and night, sea and land,
their hollow souls
lightly sway at a point of contact
for the universe's rotation,
like wind-bells
hanging from the corners of eaves.

인간에 비해
얼마나 축복받은 죽음인가.

해와 달, 달빛과 별빛
낮과 밤, 바다와 육지
우주 순환의 접점에서
추녀 끝 풍경처럼 가벼이 흔들리는
허허로운 너의 영혼.

Winter Mud Flat around the First Rainfall of the Year

The river flows in withdrawn silence
to seek a deeper current,
begins at long last to stretch out,
footsteps growing louder
under a layer of ice.

The winter mud flats, covered
during all of winter by snow,
are swollen with frostbite
despite the low warmth of misty sunlight.
Now struggling hard,
they raise their bodies.

In a corner of the sky,
the passage of birds, having come
across the plains of Siberia
on the romance shaping writing a poetic line.
Somewhere in the deserted place
where the birds return north,
the mud flats,
with the look of men, hair scattered, rising noisily,
one, two, three....
elbowing their way through a field
of sparse reeds, over barbed wire,

우수雨水 무렵 겨울 개펄

더 깊은 흐름 찾아
침잠된 침묵으로 흐르던 강,
모처럼 몸 푸느라
얼음장 밑 수런대는 발자국소리.

엷은 온기 실은
안개빛 햇살에도 겨우 내내 흰 눈 받아
동상으로 부풀린 겨울 개펄
들쑤시며 온 몸으로 일어선다.

하늘자락 한 켠
시詩 한 줄 긋는 낭만으로
시베리아벌판 건너온 철새들
다시금 북녘으로 회귀하는
휑뎅그렁한 공간 어디쯤서
개펄은
부석대며 일어서는 쑥부쟁이 사내들 몰골로
하나, 두울, 세엣...
철조망 너머 성긴 갈대숲 헤치고
아직은 손끝 에이는 강물로 다가선다.

땟국 전 시커먼 거적때기 걸친

to approach the river water, still biting cold.

Like a procession of the homeless
wrapped in pieces of dirty straw mats,
the mud flats hide their faces to the last....

노숙자露宿者 행렬처럼

끝내 얼굴을 숨긴 채...

Midwinter

Dreary news came to my breakfast table
Remicon trucks packing
the surrounds of Danyang Cement Factory
had disappeared for the first time in thirty years.

Even if the subway suddenly stops
during rush hour in dark tunnel
between Shinlim and Bongchon stations,
no one asks why.

Those warriors who, about this time last year,
Threaded passages of the transfer station,
Flags fluttering, demanding their corporate dismissal
be reversed,
Where have they gone?

"We were rather happier during our struggle,
Our place at present looks like Auschwitz..."

The tower crane, once used to build high-rises,
stopped dead, and underneath,
all sorts of rubbish
trampled on, broken, torn, or upset.

대한大寒

삼십 년래 처음으로
단양시멘트공장 주변 그득 채웠던
레미콘트럭이 자취를 감춰버렸다는
적막한 뉴스가 아침식탁에 날아들었다.

신림, 봉천역 사이 캄캄한 굴속에서
느닷없이 출근길 전철이 멈춰서도
왜 멈췄는지 이유를 묻는 사람은 없다.

작년 이맘때
정리해고 철회 깃발 나부끼며 저벅저벅
환승역 통로를 누비던 전사들은
대체 어디로 사라져버린 것일까.

투쟁할 때가 차라리 행복했어
아우슈비츠가 따로 있는 게 아냐

높은 빌딩 올리던 타워크레인 작동 멈춘
그 아래 밟히느니 부서지고, 깨어지고, 엎어진
잡동사니

나라살림 맡은 나라님들
어느 날 갑자기 나라를 몽땅 거덜내 놓고
사표 한 장 내는 마지막 양심마저 실종된

In the center of winter
Those government officials in charge
suddenly, one day, bankrupted the country,
but discarded even the conscience
to submit their resignation, all the same, not even one.

The heavy snows that invaded at night
like IMF's dreadful occupation.

The group dancing in the void
looks just like a comic illustration.

이 겨울 한 복판,
밤사이 IMF 점령군처럼 쳐들어온 폭설暴雪.

코미디 삽화만 같은 허공 속 춤추는 군무群舞.

Secondhand Bookstore

Oh! you survived
and managed to come here.

Your body, chosen
then discarded.

Unable to receive the basic price
for your body because of the original sin
you once married,
your face hanging without make-up,
and I see a face
sometimes abandoned after short marriage.

Nevertheless, how fortunate it is
That you survived,
to participate under your own name
in a dogfight to be sold
even at a quarter of the fixed price...

Though almost completely forgotten by people,
you may compete alongside best sellers
that once raised the price of paper,
and look forward to a stroke of good luck
as some person with good eyes

중고서점

용케 살아나
예까지 왔구나.

택함을 받았다가
버려진 몸.

한 때 시집장가 들었던 원죄로
받아야 할 기본몸값도 받지 못하고
화장기 없이 내걸린 얼굴,
더러 신혼에 소박맞은 얼굴도 보이누나.

그래도 얼마나 다행이랴
이렇게라도 살아남아
반에 반값에나마
팔려나갈 수 있는 난전에
이름 석 자나마 내걸 수 있다는 것이...

비록 너는 세상 사람들 기억에 아득하지만
한 때 낙양의 지가를 올린 베스트셀러와도 나란히
어깨를 겨루고 있고
아직도 감춰진 보물을 찾아 헤매는
눈 밝은 이도 있어
행여나 하는 요행수를 바라볼 수도 있으니...

wanders about seeking hidden jewels...

The heroine, brave without rival,
Who exposed, racily, the erogenous zones
asleep deep within the body, who said
"I also sometimes wish to be the star in a porno",
is also on sale as a secondhand
due to the irresistible passage of time.

몸 속 깊이 잠자는 성감대를 야하게도 펼쳐 보인
'나도 때로는 포르노그래피의 주인공이 되고 싶다'
그 용감무쌍한 여주인공도
어쩔 수 없는 세월 앞에
중고 세일되고 있다.

How to Write a Poem

A woman is beautiful
when she remains
an object to be looked at.

Blank space that provides distance,
That unsatisfied, regretful aesthetic.

However, as soon as one approaches
to meet, face to face,
the eager yearning ends
Only dry prose remains.

시법詩法

여자는 바라보는 대상으로
머물러 있을 때 아름답다.

거리가 갖는 여백,
그 아쉬움의 미학美學.

다가가 만나는 순간
그리움은 끝나고
산문散文만 남는다.

Felt Hat

- longing for my bereaved father

Though softly covered by the shade of a broad-brimmed
hat,
his youth and lenient smiles showing
to the world.
Even during the desperation of the late 1950s,
my father's figure was dazzling,
a hope for our family.

Even in the twenty-first century,
fin-de-siecle despair remains unchanged,
my desperate hope
to go through its way
with my children who still so young.

As if cherishing the young lover
From black-and-white films of the past,
Father,
I, now middle-aged,
Revisited Rhine River after 20 years.
Standing on the riverbank, I recalled
your younger days, those years I could hardly remember.

I placed your brilliant hope and romance,
On my forehead.

중절모자
- 돌아가신 아버님을 기리며

차양 넓은 그늘에 설핏 가려도
온 세상 향해 드러나던 젊음과 넉넉한 웃음,
50년대 말 절망적이었던 상황에서도
아버님 모습은 우리 가족의 희망처럼 눈부셨다.

21세기에도 세기말적 절망은 여전하고
아직도 여리디 여린 자식들과 함께
헤쳐 나가야 할 절실한 희망.

흘러간 흑백영화 속
사랑을 나누던 청춘남녀를 추억하듯이
아버님,
어느 덧 중년이 된 저는
20년 만에 다시 찾은 유럽 라인강변에서
결코 꺾일 수 없었던 아버님의
아득한 그 시절을 떠올리며
젊은 당신의 눈부신 희망과 낭만을 제 이마에 얹었습니다.

Memory on Kim Sungchoon, Senior Poet*

The fresh scent of soil
nearby a thousand-year-old royal tomb.

Passing through blades of grass at dawn
on which brilliant drops of morning dew have formed,
he ascends a thousands years as a salmon,
becoming younger than before.

On his back, the limitlessly dim
Fields of Shilla Kingdom,
to his chest, he embraces Namsan Mountain
where all sorts of Buddhist statues breathe alive.
Near the edge of his right shoulder,
He places, like a medal, *Nangsan Mountain
Where Queen Sunduk rests,
He fell asleep happily.

The poet takes a stroll in an open field,
a puppy leading his way at sunset,
he pulls those ancient livings from the realm of
unconsciousness, free from fixed idea,
to exchange words and feelings...

Returning back to those early days, so far distant times,
only violent rain and wind could be seen,
confronting war just like severe storm

성춘형 생각

천년고도 왕릉 곁
푸릇푸릇 흙냄새
새벽 영롱한 아침이슬 영근 풀섶 헤치며
한 마리 연어로 천년 세월 거슬러 올라
더욱 젊어진 그는
뒷벌에는 끝 간 데 없어
더욱 아스라한 신라의 들판을
앞가슴에는 오만 가지 불상
살아 숨 쉬는 남산을 품고 산다.

오른 쪽 어깨 언저리쯤
선덕여왕이 잠든 *낭산狼山을 훈장처럼 붙이고
잠자리에 든다.

무념무상 무위의 경지에서 그네들을 끌어내
말과 정을 주거니 받거니 하는 그는
일몰이면 강아지 한 마리 앞장 세워
너른 벌판으로 산책을 나선다.

천지가 개벽하던 아득한 시절
거친 바람 몰아치던,
살기 위해 죽고 죽여야 하는
전쟁의 와중에
오롯이 당간지주와 주춧돌만 남은

where men killed to survive or were killed,
He, like a medium having those days,
restores brilliant imagination
at a ruined temple site where
only stone pillars and foundations remain.

He embraces, strokes a painful history
from wretchedly collapsed with a loud shriek,
on the remnants of broken tiles.

From a kite someone has loosed in an open field,
he deduces the wisdom
of Kim Yushin's burning kite, the great general of Shilla
who quelled a rebellion.
Through his singular ear and heart,
he hears the beating of horse hooves
running to Goguryo and Baekje Kingdom,
with heroes and nameless soldiers
on their backs.

If you take a walk with him at sunset,
you can truly see, with ease and curiosity,
that flocks of birds, seeking their nests
without any sense of direction,
stay a while to fly
in a circle, over his head.

---

* Kim Sungchoon, senor poet who made his debut with the poem 'Listening to Bach music' by recommendation of poet Park, Mokwol.
* Nangsan : long stretched hill in the shape of cocoon wherein the first woman King in Korean history, Sunduk(AD 580~647) tomb is located.

폐허의 절터에서
그는 때를 만난 무당처럼
화려한 상상력을 복원한다.

깨어진 기왓장 흔적에서
와르르르 외마디 비명 지르며
처절히 무너져 내린
아픈 역사를 껴안고 어루만진다.

누군가 너른 벌판에 띄워 올린 연에서
모반謀叛을 진압한 김유신의
불붙은 연의 지혜를 이끌어내고
고구려 백제로 치닫던
영웅과 이름없는 군사들 말발굽소리
그만의 귀와 가슴으로 듣는다.

해 저물녘
그와 함께 길을 나서면
보금자리 찾아 방향 없이 떠돌던 새떼들이
한 동안 그의 머리 위를 떠나지 않고
원을 그리는 것을
참으로 편안하고 신기한 마음으로 바라볼 수 있다.

---

* 김성춘 : 작품 '바하를 들으며' 로 목월선생 추천을 받아 등단한 〈심상〉
　　　　1회 선배 시인
* 낭산(狼山) : 누에고치 모양의 얇고 긴 언덕 모양의 산으로 신라시대 한국 최초의 여왕인
　　　　선덕여왕 무덤이 있다.

Guchondong Valley of Muju

Where are you hiding
your young and beautiful figure?

Unhindered mountain stream,
spinning round, overflowing, breaking,
frightened into paleness.
The day when I portended
approaching of fate,
an auditory hallucination
amid boisterous laughter
like a pair of white Korean sock.
A crying sound, sorrowful almost bestial.

Where have you gone?
Did you leisurely disappear into that forest,
Having leaped thirty-five lonely years
as nimbly as a pole vaulter?
It is hard to guess when the way through
thick forest will become impassable
from overgrown weed,
and the valley, once radiant with our youth,
now parallel lines, side-by-side
was changed to newly paved road.

Long, broken branch of an ash tree lying

무주구천동

어디쯤 그대 젊고 아름다운 모습 감추고 있는가.

휘저어 돌아가 울울 콸콸 넘치고 깨지며
하얗게 소스라치는 저 거침없는 계곡물,
하얀 버선 같은 눈 시린 깔깔 웃음 결에
환청으로 다가오는
운명을 예감하던 그날, 짐승 같던 서러운 울음.

어딜 갔는가?
그대
외로운 35년 세월 장대높이뛰기 선수같이
훌쩍 뛰어넘어 유유히 저 숲속으로 사라졌는가.
울울 창창 계곡 사잇길,
무성한 잡초로 끊긴 날조차 가늠하기 어렵고
우리의 젊음으로 찬연했던 계곡은
신작로 같은 길로 이제 나란히 걷는 평행선이 되었구나.

물푸레나무 가지 꺾이어 길게 누운 계곡물의 정지된 흐름
푸른 세월은 서서히 삭아가고
그대 한번쯤 그리움 쏟으려 이곳을 찾기는 하였는지?

물레방아 도는 객사客舍에서 함께 깨어나
싸리울타리 너머 한가롭게 올려다 보았던
아득한 외줄기 산길의 끝점 백련암,

across the stream, stopping its flow.
The time of vitality is slowly decaying.
Did you once visit, urged by longing?

Awakening at an inn with a waterwheel,
we looked, leisurely, over a wall of bush clovers,
at Baeknyonam Temple
located at the end of a distant mountain pass.
Now, stepped on and kicked by large crowds,
it has risen like a tall gate,
losing its quiet and stillness.

When I picked up a skipping stone I had used
to play with my young son,
its eyes, nose, mouth, ears washed away
by wind and frost, but the contours of its lovely face
miraculously survived, and my hot palm filled
with fresh tears.

Oh, how I miss you!
as if I never met you
despite already met in our lifetime,
because, like a fairy who descended from heaven
on a moonlit night, you have gone,
leaving just your youth, like a white gem.

That sublime orchestral concerto suddenly
rushes onto my back as I leave the valley,
soars high into the sky in a flash!

이젠 밟히고 채이는 무리들로 솟을대문처럼 솟구쳐 올라
고즈넉한 모습 찾을 길 없구나.

동행한 어린 아들과 물수제비 뜨던 조약돌 주워 드니
눈 코 입 귀 풍상에 씻겼어도
곱디고운 얼굴선은 기적같이 살아남아
뜨거운 손아귀 가득 새삼 눈물 자아내누나

오, 그리운 그대
살아생전 만나도 만난 것 같지 않은 것 같음은
달밤에 내려온 선녀같이
그대 백옥의 젊음을 이곳에 두고 그대로 떠났음이려니...

계곡을 떨치고 떠나는 등 뒤로 왈칵 다가서다
돌연 하늘로 솟구쳐 오르는 저 장엄한 오케스트라 협주곡.

Daegwanryong* Mountain

The one who wears a crown is lonely, but fragrant.

On a desolate mountain path,
like a man hardly to breathe, lacking oxygen,
I float lightly
as if I were light single point touching the sky

The sea, lying down, brings
Similarly shaped ridges together
with the tips of its feet, yet
Is helplessly confined
at the end of the mountain range.
The profuse chorus of insects covers the green meadow,
While the bellowing of lazy milk cows
sometimes respond,
Shaking the dawn to lay and soothe
The lazy day that has begun.

As each blade of grass, like a newborn baby,
cries toward the sky with vigor,
the valley, hurriedly rushing to the river and sea,
raises the clamorous buzz of its stream.

On the edge of Maebong's* peak,

대관령*

관冠 쓴 자는 외롭다. 그러나 향기롭다.

산소 결핍 무호흡증 걸린 사람처럼 적막한 산길,
하늘에 맞닿은 나는 점 하나로 둥둥 떠가고 있다.

길게도 누운 저 먼 발치 끝
고만고만한 산등성 아우르는 바다는
산맥 끝에 꼼짝없이 갇혀 있다.
푸른 초원을 뒤덮은 풍성한 풀벌레 합창.
이따금 화답하는 게으른 젖소울음 새벽을 흔들어
또 다시 시작되는 게으른 하루를 곁에 뉘어 달랜다.
신생아 같은 풀잎만이 올올한 기상으로 잎잎이
하늘 향해 외치자
계곡이 강, 바다로 서둘러 달음박질치는
저 부산스런 물발자국소리

짙은 숲 그늘 이룬 매봉 정상 언저리 핸드폰도 끊기고 만다.
큰 문은 더 이상 문이 아니다 활짝 열린 하늘이다 구름이다
바람이다 새다 말이다 곤충이다 물이다 야생화다 꿈꾸는
한 마리 젖소다
무한적막 아침,

cell phones receive no signal.

The large door is no longer a door,
It would be open sky, cloud, wind,
bird, horse, insect, water, a wild flower,
sometimes, milk cow who dreams his own world.

In the infinitely lonesome, quiet morning,
I can hear the sound of a single cloud in the sky
stretching.

---

* meaning of Daegwanryong; Large Door Mountain, Maebong: Falcon mountain

* This poem was recited by the author on the train in the opening ceremony for
Seoul outskirt circulation train by Korea National Railway Co. and broadcasted
by MBC-TV in early 2000.

한 점 구름이 기지개 켜는 소리를 듣는다.

* 이 시는 2000년대 초 서울 교외선 순환열차 opening기념열차 event에서 저자에 의해 낭송되었으며 MBC-TV로 방영되었음.

The Palace of Nirvana

Having passed Sangwonsa Temple
on Odaesan Mountain,
heavenly garden with which a lonely cloud
plays, I entered a mountain path
leading up Birobong Mountain.
Then, on a knoll far removed,
where deep shade of a thick pine forest
presses down heavily,
I saw a Buddhist temple soaring all alone.

Without people's sticky attachment to objects,
as persistent and base as passion,
without decorations most childish,
desolate landscape,
like a bottomless abyss,
all the more free
in its endlessness.

Resonance box, which filters transparently
and reechoes all sounds for eternity,
the sound of a breeze through a pine grove,
of mountain birds,
of a valley stream,
of wind chimes in silvery sunlight,

적멸보궁寂滅寶宮

구름 한 자락 더불어 노니는
천상天上의 정원, 오대산 상원사上院寺 거쳐
비로봉 오르는 산길 저만큼 비겨나
솔숲 짙은 그늘 발등에 무겁게 뒤채는
산자락 둔덕에
외딴 절 한 채 솟구쳐 있었네.

애욕愛慾처럼 집요하고 추한
인간들의 끈끈한 물질의 집착,
유치찬란한 치장 없어
외려 홀빈한
저 무궁무진無窮無盡
끝 모를 심연 같은 적막강산

솔바람, 산새, 계곡물소리
은빛 햇살가루 찰랑이는 풍경소리
억겁億劫의 소리란 소리 죄다
투명하게 걸러 되울림 하는
공명共鳴상자
허허로운 주변 싸고도는 저 목탁소리조차
무겁다.

전생과 이승과 내세
윤회輪回의 한복판에 가부좌 틀고

even the wooden gong,
spinning around the hollow insides,
feels heavy.

Maitreya, sitting cross-legged
amid the cycle of reincarnation,
of his past life, this life, and next one,
A butterfly that, hatching from its cocoon, seeks to
ascend to heaven of highest level.

Oh! the butterfly who is about to be hatched to lift up
to heaven,
breaking though a cocoon.

True freedom finally to be gained
Through total destruction
until all belongings are destroyed.

도솔천에 간 미륵이 우화등선羽化登仙하려
고치를 뚫고 마악 부화하는 나비,

멸滅해야 비로소 얻게 되는 참자유.

Autumn

Autumn does not decay,
but ripened while decaying.

Knowing right time when it should go,
It quietly heads towards the soil,
A docile gesture that reflects
wisdom of its fate.

The nothingness of existence
as it disappears entirely from the ground,
sinking into the soil as a rotten leaf
after rolling about on the surface.

Long-awaited rest
staying for a while with fallen leaves,
the strong sunlight that ripen fruits...

Peaceful death
sinking slowly and steadily in a marsh of gathered light.

가을

가을은 지는 것이 아니라
저물면서 여무는 것입니다.

자신이 가야할 때를 알아
조용히 땅으로 향하는
지천명知天命의 순한 몸짓.
잠시 땅위에 뒹굴다 썩은 낙엽으로
흙속에 스며들어
지상에서 온전히 사라지는
존재의 허무.

과실果實을 익히는 여문 햇살
낙엽과 함께 머무는
모처럼의 안식

고인 빛의 늪에 서서히 빠져드는
평화로운 죽음.

A Bamboo Grove Sits on Eggs

The dim mountain path
where the heat shimmers brightly.
The bamboo grove suddenly noisy
mixed with sounds of wind and chirping birds.

Splendid dancing spring sunlight,
Wavering between thick shades.

In a steep, dangerous slope,
oh! each bird bears a plump egg
depending on the wind as a nest.

대숲은 알을 품고 있다

아지랑이 아롱아롱 아련한 산길,
바람소리, 우짖는 새소리
부쩍 소란스러워진 대숲

짙은 그늘 틈새 얼비치는
저 봄빛의 현란한 춤.

위태로운 비탈,
바람을 둥지삼아 새들은
뱃속마다 토실토실 알을 품고 있구나!

Summer

Coo.... Coo.... Coo....
A ringdove enlarging infinitely,
a large, crying sound box,
swallows the whole mountain
and burrows into my heart,
which has nothing left to hide.

Blinded by palpitating curiosity,
we took to the woods,
but there was no place on earth
where two bodies, like dust specks, could find to cover.
We left after having tussled
with shyness between us,
near the stump of a pine tree, awkwardly tilted.
The low spur of a hill, dim beyond memory.

Around this time,
under the shade of dense, dark blue, young pines,
like a pomegranate, over-ripened and bursting red inside,
you may even throw away shyness
suffering from a hot fever.

여름

구우~구우~구
커다란 울음의 공명상자 한없이 키우고 있는
산비둘기 한 마리
온 산을 삼키며
더 이상 숨길 것 없는 내 마음까지 파고 듭니다.

두근거리는 호기심에 앞이 캄캄해
숲속 찾아들었으나
천지사방 티끌 같은 두 몸 가릴 곳 없어
어설프게 비탈진 소나무 등걸 언저리에서
부끄러움 사이에 두고 실랑이만 벌이다
홀쩍 떠나버린 가물가물 기억 저편 야트막한 산모퉁이.

이맘때쯤이면
촘촘이 돋아난 검푸른 잔솔 그늘 아래
여물다 못해 속내마저 빨갛게 터져버린 석류
부끄러움마저 벗어 던지고
뜨거운 몸살 앓고 있겠지요.

Dog Day (Mid Summer)

The shrill chirping of a cicada
bites off a piece of summer
as red as flesh of watermelon.
The monotonous tune in high octave
is ripening into black seed.

One sound calls another sound
at last, locks up
the rough summer.

The cicada stops singing as if exhausted
after pushing the full moon
high into the sky over a roof cooked by summer heat.
Then, all kinds of insects
recover their own voice.

The whole world is so cool and fresh
as if cold water were poured on its back.

중복中伏

수박 속살 같은
붉은 여름 한 자락 베어 물고
매암매암 찌르르르~
옥타브 드높은 단음조單音調
까아만 씨알로 영글고 있다.

소리는 소리를 불러
마침내 난폭한 여름마저
가두어 버리고 마는구나.

더위로 익은 지붕 너머 만월滿月을
힘겹게 중천中天까지 밀어올리고
기진氣盡하듯 울음 멈추자
비로소 뭇 풀벌레
제 목소리 되찾고

온 천지는
등물한 듯 시원타.

Cosmic Fete in the Night Sky

As I was about to go to bed,
a brilliant star, over an attic window
touching the sky,
sent me a flashing signal.
It was a marvelous occurrence.

Though I heard of stars twinkling,
it was the first time that
a star flashed at me.

Was it because of the full moon,
unusually bright today,
that I discerned for the first time
the signal sent by the star?

Awakening alone in hushed silence
Late at night when all the world slept,
I looked again at the sky.
The Belt of Orion and the Great Bear,
affectionate, as if about to touch,
were twinkling in the center of the sky,
but it was the full moon, being nearest to earth,
that lit up the night most brightly.

밤하늘 우주잔치

잠자리 들 무렵
하늘 맞닿은 다락방 창 너머
밝은 별 하나
깜빡 신호를 보내왔습니다.
정말 신기한 일입니다.

별이 반짝인다는 말 들었어도
이렇게 저를 향해 반짝반짝 반짝인 것은
처음입니다.

오늘 따라 유난히 밝은 보름달 탓에
별이 보내는 교신을
비로소 알게 된 것일까요.

밤 깊어 삼라만상 모두 잠든
고요한 적막 속 홀로 깨어나
다시금 하늘 보니
삼형제별 나란히 박힌 오리온좌, 북두칠성
맞닿을 듯 정답게
하늘 한복판 유난히 반짝이는데
그 하늘을 훤히 밝히는 건
바로 지구와 가장 가까운 보름달이었습니다.

오늘 저 달이 커든 눈부신 등불

I came to know, for the first time,
that the brilliant lamp lit by the moon
embraces the universe tenderly
and, infusing the stars with life, lets them whisper
their own sweet nothings in the night sky.

Secret whispers in the vast stillness
where calm peace dwells, all too different
from the vortex of war swallowing earth.

When I looked again,
the star that sent me the signal
no longer winked at me, they
were indulging in a fete by themselves,
were shining with their eyes full of brightness.

우주를 한 아름 포근히 끌어안고
별빛들에게 생명을 불어넣어
밤하늘에서 저들끼리 만의 아늑한 밀어 속삭인다는 것
비로소 알았습니다.

전쟁의 소용돌이에 휘말린 지구와는
너무나 다른 안온한 평화 깃들여 있는
광활한 정적 속 밀어.

다시금 살펴보니
교신을 보내온 그 별도
이젠 더 이상 내게 눈짓 주지 않고
저들끼리의 잔치에 흥건히 젖어들어
마냥 총기 서린 눈동자
반짝이고 있었습니다.

Vine of Ivy

Hanging a rope
on a remote vertical wall.

Wriggling on a single navel chord,
leaves and stalks take turns
competing one another.

The road to the sky has been opened,
Stridingly, skillfully like Spiderman,
By fully stretching its tiny hands
taking short breaths at each steep, strategic point,

By feeding the wind stealing into the dense shade,
tens of thousands of ray-like kites,
raised to look truly alike,
are made to float gently
in shape of towering mass clouds
where peace and rest of the earth dwells.

Dazzling whisper, seeming to
reach even the rooftop
where the sunlight has fully ripened,
You sway lightly,
as if eternity comes and goes
between light and shadow.

담장이 넝쿨

아득한 직립直立의 벽에
자일을 건다.

탯줄 하나로 꿈틀꿈틀
잎 줄기 앞서거니 뒤서거니 다투는 사이

강파른 길목마다 잔 호흡 고르며
앙증맞은 손바닥 한껏 펼쳐
스파이더맨같이 성큼성큼
용케 하늘길 열었구나.

짙은 그늘 숨어든 바람결만으로
참 고르게도 키워놓은
수천수만 가오리 연鳶
지상의 평화, 안식 깃든 뭉게구름으로
더덩실 피워 올렸어라.

햇살 무르익은 지붕 위에까지
저렇듯 눈부신 속살거림,
빛과 그림자 사이
영원永遠의 시간 오가듯
하늘하늘 하늘대고 있누나.

The Chestnut Blossoms Bloomed

One day you unexpectedly appeared to me.

Embracing the wind to my chest on a hill,
I flew a kite high in the sky
late night, I also attempted
to connect soundlessly by e-mail towards you

It is not that no news arrives.
You are not the figure in the landscape.
If I wish to be closer to you, you are always approachable.
However, I will never know you.

I burn myself every night
as an incombustible tree stump,
thus caused inhale acrid smoke,
pour hopeless tears.

One day in June,
unable to endure the dazzling day,
I went to the riverbank with my friend.
Laughing heartily with a group
that kept pleasant time on a double-headed drum,
the pebbles, strikingly glistening,
pricked my eye.

밤꽃이 피었어요

어느 날 문득 당신이 보였어요.

언덕에 올라 바람을 가슴에 안고
높다랗게 연을 올리고
밤늦은 때는 e메일로 소리없는 접속을
시도해 보았지요.

소식이 오지 않는 것도 아니고
풍경 속의 모습도 아닌데
가까이하려면 언제나 가까이할 수 있는 당신인데
도무지 당신을 알 수가 없네요.

그래 저는 밤마다 불연소不燃燒 나무 등걸로 타오르며
난데없이 매캐한 연기만 마시고 속절없는 눈물을
쏟아내고 있습니다.

6월 어느 날
눈부신 하루를 견딜 수 없어
친구와 강가에 나갔습니다.
장구에 장단 맞춘 패거리들과 깔깔거리며
유쾌하게 지낸 강가에는
조약돌이 유난히도 반짝거리며 눈을 찔렀습니다.

그곳에는 하늘을 이고 수도 없이 무수한 밤꽃이

There, carrying the sky on their head,
a countless number of fresh, yellow chestnut blossoms
bloomed,
soaking my heart.

Do you know me
who helplessly drunken by so strong fragrance...

샛노랗게 핀 걸,
그 흥건히 저리는 밤꽃향기를 한껏 마시고
속절없이 취한 저를
그대는 아시는지?

Brother

Born a year apart, Moonjin and Woojin
are rivals during their lifetime.
However, like twin,
they unite firmly before a common enemy.

Sometimes the younger one threatens and scares
those who maliciously ridiculed his elder brother,
then, mischievously, plays innocent.

He detests the scolding from adults
that obstructs his free, unfettered prospect,
never accept to being called a good and polite child.

As long as open road is before them,
even if their homeworks pile up,
They still prefers to run outdoor,
Both are cosmic warriors with explosive passion
on Starcraft in computer games playing shop.

Drawing up historical figures
such as Wang-gun[*1], Goong-ye[*2],
those from the Three Kingdoms[*3]
confronting the elder with a wooden sword,
the younger bursts into tears

형제

연년생 문진 우진이는
평생 라이벌
그러나 공동의 적 앞에서는 똘똘 뭉치는
쌍둥이 닮은 꼴.

때로는 심술궂게 형을 놀려대는
형 친구를 어르고 겁주다가
개구쟁이처럼 짐짓 시침 떼기도 한다.

자유분방한 앞길 막는
어른들 잔소리,
예절바른 착한 어린이란 굴레는 딱 질색.

가야할 길이 먼 만큼
해야 할 숙제도 쌓이지만
아직은 뛰노는 게 더 즐겁고
PC방 스타크라프트게임에
폭발적인 열정 드러내는 우주전사.

삼국지, 왕건, 궁예 역사 속 인물을 끌어내
겁 없이 나무칼로 맞서다가
형의 역습에 울음보 터뜨리지만
소낙비 그치자 맑은 하늘 내밀 듯
아무렇찮은 표정.

from his elder brother's counterattack,
but soon displays an indifferent expression
like a clear sky revealed
as soon as the Summer shower end.

Whenever they get up late,
they scramble to grow taller
by the span of a hand.
This Summer, they appear quite grown-up
enough to leave their parent
for a year or more
to reside overseas.

Open road ahead both of you
unhindered future like wind.

---

*1 Wang-gun: the founder of the Koryo Kingdom, which lasted for more than five
    hundred years in Korea.
*2 Goong-ye: the founder of the short-lived Taebong Kingdom in Korea.
*3 The Three Kingdoms Story: one of the most famous historical novels in China.

늦잠 잘 때마다 한 뼘씩 앞다퉈 크는 키
한 일년쯤 부모와 떨어져
해외 홈스테이도 할 수 있을 만큼
올 여름 제법 어른스러워졌구나.

바람처럼 거침없는 너희들의 앞길.

▪ 왕건 : 500년 이상 지속된 고려 왕조 창건자
▪ 궁예 : 태봉왕국 창건자
▪ 삼국지 : 중국의 저명한 역사소설

Moonjin's Race along with His Shadow

Eye, nostril, ear, mouth…
Seven holes of the body are opened
On, seven times seven, forty-ninth day.
The day passed with eyes opened
by thoughtful grandfather's awakening.

Toddling persistently becomes brave
after first birthday.

"Ready .... Go!"
Mimicking words,
tightly clenching tiny hands,
the boy does not stop racing
from the veranda to the sink of apartment.

One mild, winter afternoon
he went out with his father
having carefully watched his shadow
accompany him down the road,
he began to play with it,
using his tiny arms, feet, and gestures.

Regardless of narrow wide space,
high, low stairs,
morning, noon, evening, night,

문진이의 그림자달리기

눈, 코, 귀, 입...
몸 속 7개 구멍 죄 뚫린다는
7 7 49일을
자상한 할아버지 일깨움 속에 지나고

첫돌 지나자
부쩍 씩씩해지는 걸음마

"요이~~ 땅!"
말시늉까지 하며
조막지 주먹 불끈 움켜쥐고
아파트 베란다에서 싱크대까지
달리기를 쉬지 않는 아이.

푸근한 겨울 오후
아빠 따라 길 나섰다가
함께 길동무하는 제 그림자
조심스레 지켜보다가
앙증스런 팔 다리 몸짓
그림자놀이를 시작한다.

좁고 넓은 공간
높고 낮은 계단
아침 점심 저녁 밤낮 가리지 않고

under sunlight, moonlight, starlight
even artificial light, everywhere,
he played excitedly with his shadow.

The shadow, casting sidelong glance,
takes the lead, sometimes follows,
but, always clinging to his feet,
never separates from him.

It follows him, then stops,
having hesitated awhile,
starts to run with him.
How curious for him to play along with the shadow!

Though a sudden obstacle
caused him to fall or break,
his running never stops.

Nervous about him to be hurt by a car,
his father, measuring his eyes
sometimes in a hurried pace,
turns him about-face, like turning
toy soldier wounded spring,
lifts up to stop him,
but Moonjin never ceases running with his shadow.

His footsteps are interminable,
carried on centrifugal force
like a train running endless track,

햇빛 달빛 별빛 불빛 아래
어디서고 벌리는 신나는 그림자놀이.

힐끗 곁눈질로
앞서가며 때로는 따라오기도 하는
그러나 늘상 발에 매달려
떨어지지 않는 그림자.

따라오다 멈춰서고
멈칫거리다 함께 달리는
신기한 그림자놀이.

갑자기 나타난 장애물에
넘어지고 깨져도
그칠 줄 모르는 달음박질

차에 다칠까
조마조마해진 아빠는 눈어림으로
때로는 급한 발걸음으로
태엽 감은 장난감 병정 되돌려 놓듯
아이를 돌려 세우고
덥석 안아 말리기도 하지만
문진이는 그림자와 함께
달리기를 멈추지 않는다.

지구의 반경마저 좁은 듯
무한궤도 달리는 열차처럼
원심으로 무한정 치닫는 발걸음.

as if the earth's radius is too short.

Even if his knees grazed when falling,
his forehead broken from impact,
his face scratched by thorny vines,
he continues to play with his shadow,
never stop in his sweet sleep.

Moonjin's calves became,
round and strong, so soon
like hardy, ripened oranges.

넘어져 까진 무릎
부딪쳐 깨진 이마
가시넝쿨 긁힌 얼굴로
달디단 잠속에서까지 달리는 그림자놀이.

어느 새 문진이 장딴지는
탱자열매 익듯
탱글탱글 영글었구나.

For a Beautiful and Lonely Soul

- In Memory of Professor Shin, Kee-chul, The City Graduate
  School, Hanyang University

For 38 years we were close
As if he were my brother
So sorrowfully he died at 10:30 on May 11th, 2001,
from his second cerebral hemorrhage.

He, unable to let go of my yearning
with grief, visited twice afterwards
in the form of his soul.

He first appeared to me at dawn
20 days after his burial.
Before the majestic sea
where white foam broke against breakwater,
his voice, overwhelming sounds of waves,
conveyed his gratitude
to friends who had sent their condolences,
while asking me to look after his bereaved family,
regretfully disappeared like last scene of cinema.

I had visited his tomb
at Cheonan public cemetery
for the rite of 49th day after his death,
there I called his name longingly,
like the song of spiritual invocation

아름답고 외로운 영혼을 위하여

- 한양대학교 도시대학원 신기철교수를 추모하며

38년간 친형제 같은 정을 나눈 그가
2001년 5월11일 10시30분 두 번째 뇌출혈로 세상을 떠난 후
그리움과 애달픈 마음을 떨치지 못하는 내게
그는 두 번 영혼의 모습으로 찾아왔다.

첫 번째는 땅속에 그를 묻은 지 20일쯤 지난
새벽녘에 나타났다.
하얀 포말이 격정적으로 방파제에 부서지는
웅혼한 바다를 앞세우고
그는 파도소리에 자신의 목소리를 또렷이 실어
문상 온 친구들에 대한 고마움을 전하면서
남은 가족에 대한 걱정과 부탁을 하곤 아쉽게 사라져갔다.

두 번째는 49제祭때 천안공원묘지에 묻힌 그의 산소를 찾아
소월素月의 초혼가招魂歌처럼
이승과 저승의 한없는 간극을 메우려 애타게 그를 부르며
그가 고등학교 때 쓴 수필 '못 다한 그리움'을
젖은 울음으로 낭송하고
그의 넋을 위무慰撫한 직후 꿈 속에서였다.

그는 저녁 무렵 번화한 길 건너편에서
몸체는 어둠에 가려 보이지 않은 채
잔잔하나 밝게 웃는 얼굴을 세 번 나를 향해
드러냈다가 이내 스러져갔다.

written by Sowol, a Korean distinguished poet,
trying to fill the infinite gulf
between this world and world after life.
I read aloud with tears flowing down my cheeks,
'The Unfinished Longing',
an essay he had written in high school,
wholeheartedly wishing to console his soul.

In that evening,
on the other side of the crowded street,
he revealed his face to me three times,
with his body buried in the dark, invisible,
smiling quietly but brightly,
and soon vanished.

When I confirmed his appearance
to friends nearby, surprisingly
he continued to manifest his face.

Since then, he has no more shown himself to me.
Is he quietly looking down on this world,
his face cleanly washed
with pity, but pure and clear sensitivity,
from that distant star discovered by Saint-Exubery
where a little prince lives?

내가 놀라움으로 옆 친구들에게 그의 모습을 확인시키자
그는 계속 자신의 얼굴을 증명해 보였다.

그 후로 모습을 드러내지 않고 있는 그는
생떽쥐베리가 발견한 저 우주 공간
어린 왕자가 사는 별나라에서
애처롭게 그러나 순수하고 맑은 감성으로
말갛게 씻긴 얼굴로
이 지상을 그윽이 내려다보고 있는 것인가.

Love Comes Like Light

Love, like light, sticks
to the very center of your heart
straight and quickly.

A single dazzling, silver arrow
that commands a halo.

Cutting off so many artificial walls,
by piercing at one's breath,
Suddenly one day,
Like a premonition come to life,
It approaches with an uneasy fluttering.

The balance weight always swaying
in empty space,
Recovering for the first time
its center of gravity,
it slowly sinks to the bottom.

Now I can see
the face of your white, clean soul,
revealed like a pebble
washed by the rapids.

사랑은 빛과 같이

사랑은 빛과 같이
곧고 빠르게
그대 가슴 한가운데 꽂힌다.

햇무리 거느린
눈부신 은빛 화살 하나.

차단된 숱한 인위의 벽
단숨에 꿰뚫고
문득 어느 날
예감의 실현처럼
설렘 안고 다가온다.

늘상 허공에 매달려
흔들리던 추
비로소 무게의 중심을 회복하며
서서히 바닥으로 가라앉고

이제야 보이누나
여울물 씻긴 조약돌처럼 드러나는
그대 해맑은 영혼의 얼굴

한 생生을 한 줄기 빛으로
아프게 부딪치며

While knocking against a lifespan
Painfully as a streak of light,
you have defended yourself wisely.

The blessing of God, bestowed upon
those who know how to wait
and how to govern the flow of time.

Today,
it is bestowed,
surrounding us
with a halo of pale light.

지혜롭게 스스로를 지켜온 그대
기다림을 알고
세월을 다스릴 줄 아는 자에게
안겨주는 신의 축복

오늘
우리 언저리를
엷은 빛살 햇무리로 번지며
안겨 오누나.

Longing -1

On a day in May
When the red royal azalea blossoms
were especially lively,
I could get no work done
for a whole day.

The crying of collared doves,
forgotten, but gathered
in a corner of my heart,
lets fly countless
futile signs that just rise up to
just beneath my chin, falling short.

I felt pain in my whole heart
Even with the rustling of leaves
as the wind passed by.

The embers that couldn't be soothed
by a mere cup of hot, coarse tea.

The measures of everyday life,
letters to be taken in by brain,
approached me as incomprehensible hieroglyphics
swelled a far like the course of a river,

그리움 -1

붉은 철쭉
유난히도 화사한
5월 한나절,
왼 종일
일이 손에 잡히지 않았다.

마음 한 켠에 고여 있던
잊었던 산비둘기 울음소리,
턱 밑까지 치받쳐 오르고
미치지 못하는
헛된 부호만 무수히 날렸다.

부스럭대는 바람결
스치는 나뭇잎소리에도
온 몸이 저려왔다.

뜨거운 엽차 한 잔으로는
결코 달랠 수 없는 불씨.

일상의 수치
머리로 새겨야하는 글자는
불가해한 상형문자로 다가와
건널 수 없는 강줄기처럼
아득히 출렁거리고

unable to be crossed.
The waves endlessly rushing
onto the castle of longing that I built.

Raising its head adamantly, the island refused
to go down under the waves.

내가 쌓은 그리움의 성城 주변으로
끝도 없이 밀려드는 파도,

한사코 섬은 고개를 쳐들고
파도 깃에 묻히려 들지 않았다.

Longing -2

A face erased
at the end of a wave.

The sideburns of the man
mending his fishing net
has grown like moss
to cover a face as dogged as a rock.

Until the white foam soaks the
Sand banks with salt crystals,
The waves draw circular arcs without pause.
The man who, with cool, sky blue eyes,
casts a net over countless bends in the current.

The blue coloring
that explodes somewhere in the abyss.

The man on a raft can no longer be seen,
but only an empty raft,
being buried in the waves,
sways on an vast chest of the sea.

그리움 - 2

파도 끝에서
지워지는 얼굴.

그물코 깁는 사내의
구레나룻은 이끼처럼 자라
바위같이 완강한 얼굴을 덮고

하얀 포말이 소금의 결정체로
모래톱을 적실 때까지
파도는 쉬임없이 호弧를 그린다.

천만갈래 물굽이에
하늘빛 서늘한 눈매로
투망질하는 사내,

심연 어디선가
폭발하는 푸른 색소.

뗏마 위 사내는 보이지 않고
파도 깃에 묻히는 빈 뗏마 하나,
드넓은 가슴 위에서 흔들리고 있다.

Reeds

Everything gathered in a row
is beautiful.

The top of a hill, all the more dazzling
because the wind and sunlight's graces
join together there.

Those nameless things
That have been discarded near and far,
Gather in armfuls here and there,
rise vigorously towards the light.

Bundle of light that shoots up spiritually
following the backwards wind,
shouting of brilliant light.

Even the tomb that lies near
becomes one with them,
So rapturous
in a glimpse of memory.

갈대

무리를 이루는
모든 것들은 아름답다.

바람과 햇살의 은총 어우러져
한결 눈부신 언덕바지

지척으로 버려져 있는
이름 없는 것들이
한 아름씩 모여
힘차게 빛을 향해
일어서는 몸짓들

역류逆流하는 바람 따라
더욱 힘차게 치솟는 빛의 다발,
현란한 빛의 아우성.

주변에 누워있는 무덤조차
한 덩이 되어
기억의 편린 속에서
황홀하다.

The National Road 7, Near to the Civilian Passage Restriction Line

Like end of a life that runs uphill
along the ridge of Taeback Mountains.
Passing by
Geojin, Gansung ports,
a hut-like checkpoint
on the passage restriction line,
the ridge of Diamond Mountain
cannot be climbed
the unfinished dream
becomes a handful of foam
sinking into the East Sea
far from Haegeumgang Rocks.

When monotonous day draws to a close,
the evening glow growing dimmer,

Suspicious footsteps
all of a sudden approach from the shadow
of a miscellaneous small trees.

The sky shuts down without warning
As if to ridicule the foolish vanguard
who shouted, "Who is it?"

7번국도 민통선 부근

태백 등줄기 따라 치달아 오른
외줄기 한 목숨의 끝
거진, 간성을 지나
움막 같은 민통선 초소를 지나
끝내 금강산 능선 기어오르지 못하고
해금강 먼 발치
동해바다 한 줌 포말로 함몰하는
다함없는 꿈.

어둑어둑 변화없는 하루
노을빛 접으며 주저 앉으면

문득
잡목 숲 그늘에서
서걱서걱 다가오는
수상한 발자국소리

어리석은 첨병의 수하誰何 비웃듯
느닷없이 닫히는 하늘
폭우로 퍼붓는 장대 같은 빗줄기
잠자는 바다 성난 파도로 일군다.

숲 사이 얼비치던 엷은 빛살마저 차단하고
첨병의 발목을 가로채며 흐르는

Great streaks of rain, pouring heavily,
raise the sleeping sea with angry waves.

The unidentified bog covered smoke and fog,
cutting off even the thin light
glimpsed from between the trees, flows while
snatching the ankles of the advancing guard.
Hostile sounds of TNT exploding
That always reverberate north
of the Demilitarized Zone, are swallowed
by the dense rain sounds
the surroundings sink into a silence
heavier than death, hit hard
by the rain defenselessly.

At long last,
one farmer's silhouette who
fortunately escaped from the passage restriction line,
is caught in the picture
screened pouring rain, wanes, leans to one side,
finally is erased with the end
of National Road No. 7.

정체모를 연무煙霧의 늪
북녘 비무장지대에서 늘상 울리는
적의의 TNT 폭음소리
자욱한 빗소리에 삼켜지고
사위는 죽음보다 무거운 침묵
무방비로 빗줄기에 강타強打당한다.

이윽고
민통선民統線을 용케 빠져나온
한 농부의 실루엣
가득한 비의 화면에 담겨
이지러져 쏠리다가
7번국도 끝과 함께 지워져 버린다.

Armed March

It merely passed by.

Stone-wall roads of the military parade,
orchard paths, lined with peach blossoms
always splendid in my memory,
small children carrying
innocent childhood on shoulder,
all things are nothing but landscape.

The higher one runs up a mountain,
the deeper a valley indulges,

Firearms destroy a pine forest
recklessly.

Unjust inheritance in our shameful history
burdened on the shoulder blades.

Volition stretches itself
at the end of what the senses can endure,
the skin flab pressed under iron helmet
erects a sharp blade on the crown of head.

When I stand on a mountaintop,

행군

스처갈 뿐이다.

열병식 돌담길도
추억 속에서 늘 화사했던
복사꽃 어우러진 과수원길도
동심을 메고 가는 조무래기들도
다만 하나의 풍경이다.

산을 치닫는 만큼
골을 깊이 빠져들고

총칼은 무작정 솔숲을 무찌른다.

어깨죽지엔
욕된 역사의 부당한 유산遺産.

감각이 인내하는 끝점에서
의지가 발돋움하고
철모 내피 밑에 눌린 군살이
정수리에 선 날을 세운다.

산정에 오르면
바람은
참으로 오랜 만에

the wind opens my windpipes
for the first time in a long run.

Nation, war, peace...
all of which I consider while
drying my sweat for a moment,
I cannot measure the end of road
I have to march.

Nobody knows.

숨통을 틔운다.
잠시 땀을 말리며
생각해 보는 민족民族 전쟁戰爭 평화平和
전진해야 할 길의 끝이 안 보인다.

아무도 모른다.

"It was a Lie!"

'Isn't it Jesus
who cloned the somatic cell of God?'

There was the right man
who made this question possible.

For a whole year in 2005
he ruled over this land
from the point of contact
between God and man.

When Kim Bongee, the ancient legendary swindler,
sold out water from the Daedong River,
there was, at least, the water itself.

However, when he attached the names
of 24 co-authors to the long tails of an article
in Science, flied abroad on
the kite named "Patient adjusted Embryonic Stem Cells"
carrying the Korean Peninsula's trademark,
not even the raw stem cells existed.

When it all crashed headlong into the ground,
a sudden turn

"뻥이야!"

'하나님 체세포를 복제한 분이
예수님이 아닐까?'
이런 의문을 가능케 해 준 사람.

2005년 한 해 그는
신과 인간의 접점에서
이 땅을 군림했다.

대동강 물 팔아먹은
봉이 김선달은
물이라는 실체라도 있었는데

24명 사이언스지 공동저자 이름을
긴 꼬리에 허수아비로 매달고
세계를 향해 띄워 올린
한반도표 〈환자맞춤형 줄기세포〉 연은
맨얼굴의 줄기세포조차 없었다.

MBC PD수첩 돌개바람에 급전직하 추락하자
서울 동숭동
세계줄기세포 허브에서 쏘아올린 뻥튀기에
4500만 국민 영문도 모른 채 밥풀 되어

Brought about by the whirlwind on MBC-TV
known as PD Notebook,
45 million Korean people,
without knowing why, were turned into fools,
the fools scattered into the empty air
launched by the World Stem Cell hub at Dongsoong-
dong, Seoul.

"It was a lie!"

허공에 흩어진다.

"뼁이야!"

Free Man

In mid of winter
The well bucket deeply
drawn each man's heart,
fathoms more deeper bottom

Mountain ranges, high and low,
suspending their vertical rise,
are joining together horizontally.

Snowflake, knowing only to land
on forest of sparse pine trees,
they began to glare with their eyes piercingly.
They strike the deep valleys, ridges,
top of Taeback Mountains,
by winding around them, circle
round and round without direction.

Having erased even the trace of
The boundaries of nature,
The time and space, already out of human control
Is truly boundless.

That unbinding free walk, gained
by throwing himself into emptiness.

자유인

저마다 가슴 속 품고 있는 두레박
깊은 곳 저울질하는
겨울 한복판

높고 낮은 산맥들
수직적 상승 멈추고
세월을 되삭임질하듯
수평적 아우름 익히고 있다.

성긴 솔숲에만 내려앉는 줄 알았던 눈발
어느 결엔가
형형한 눈빛 부릅 밝혀
저 태백준령 아득한 골짜기, 산등성, 봉우리
몰아 때리며 방향 없이 휘감아 돌고 있다.

산천경계 흔적마저 지운
초극超克의 시공時空
참으로 막막하다.

비움으로써 얻게 되는
저 거침없는 자유로운 행보.

눈과 산맥은 서로 닮은 얼굴로
어깨를 걸고

While the snow and mountain range, with like faces,
put arms around each other's shoulders,
the peaks, high and low,
surrender willingly with great cheer.

크고 작은 산봉우리들
만세 부르며 기꺼이 항복하고 있다.

Looking Up at Stars from the Chair of a Snack Stall

Where is the dream that will soak us
in this desolate city?

Stepping in while sauntering nearby,
A corner of the street stall, empty,
Seems as if it were waiting for us.

Freed from the day's fight for survival,
We transform like chameleons
and, like Nero relishing the burning of Rome,
pass our eyes over the closely displayed dead bodies
of chickens, pigs, sea squirts, sea cucumbers,
selecting and tasting what we wish.
Oh, the happy evening of salary men!

A toast, taken alone,
While looking at the lights of a high-rise apartment,
thinner than a carbide light.

The lighter our purses become
and the emptier our hearts grow,
the more earnest our unripe dream becomes.

Sitting by a shabby man in his forties,

포장마차에 앉아 별빛을 바라보며

황량한 이 도시
우리를 적셔줄 꿈은 어디 있는가.

지나치다 문득 들어서면
언제부턴가 우리를 위해 비워둔
좌판 한 귀퉁이.

진종일 생존을 위한 투쟁에서 풀려나
카멜레온처럼 변신하고
불타는 로마 완상玩賞하는 네로처럼
닭똥집, 돼지 수육, 멍게, 해삼
즐비하게 늘어선 시신屍身들을 일별하며
골라 시식하는
오, 행복한 샐러리맨의
저녁 한 때.

카바이드 불빛보다 더 여윈
고층 아파트 불빛을 바라보며
홀로 드는 축배의 잔.

주머니가 빌수록
가슴이 공허해 질수록
더욱 절실해지는 우리들의
설익은 꿈.

drinking soju, Korean liquor,
mixed with cheap soda water,
a couple of young lovers experiencing
happiness that wants nothing.
As the man vomits abusive words
abruptly into the empty air,
the couple become frightened like gun-shot deer.

Like the story of a driver
Who stepped on the accelerator
Thinking it was the brake,
Beginning some time, somewhere,
Our dream and ambition begin to veer off course.
For this, is that young couple also preparing?

The eyes of tipsy men grope the darkness
at the end of the sky.
The lower the man sits at his seat,
the more broadly the sky and stars approach
to be embraced.

Our neighbors, near and far,
plant their dreams
in each star's shadow.
swaying together
in transparent glass...

진생업을 소주에 타 마시는
초라한 40대 사내 곁에서
더없이 행복해하는 젊은 한 쌍
느닷없이 허공에 내뱉는
사내의 욕지거리에
선불 맞은 사슴 눈이 된다.

엑셀 페달을 브레이크로 잘못 알고 밟은
어느 운전기사의 사연처럼
어느 때 어디쯤서부턴가
빗나가기 시작한 우리들의 꿈과 야망
저 젊은 한 쌍도 예비하고 있을까.

취기 어린 눈은 하늘가 어둠을 더듬고
낮은 자리에 낮춰 앉을수록
더 넓게 다가와 안기는 하늘과 별들

별 그림자마다 꿈을 심고 있을
멀고 가까운 우리네 이웃들
투명한 잔속에서
함께 흔들리고...

The Road Leading to Prison

There was no one to tell me
About where it was located.

Early morning, the low, thick fog covered the road
as if to erase even the lanes.

At some corner, a road sign seemed to have
Approached and passed me by,
so I asked for directions cautiously,
but the people, silent, either shook their heads
or made hand gestures.

Arriving at a forked road, I felt
all the more embarrassed in the fog,
able to judge neither the direction nor road.

People looked afraid, and
as if turning away from a village of lepers,
went their own way in a haste.

Where even the fog suddenly disappeared,
the posts of the guardhouse towered before me
as if by magic.

However, as I got out of my car,

구치소 가는 길

그곳이 정확히 어디쯤 있는지
아무도 정확히 가르쳐주는 사람은 없었다.

이른 아침 안개는 차선마저 지우듯
자욱이 낮게낮게 깔리고

어느 모퉁이에선가
표시판이 설핏 다가왔다
사라져 간 듯도 해
조심스레 길을 물으면
사람들은 침묵 속에
고개를 흔들거나 손짓만 할 뿐

갈림길에 들어서면
안개 속에 당혹감만 더해 가고
도대체 방향, 거리를 가늠할 수 없었다.

문둥이 촌 외면하듯
사람들은 저어하며
서둘러 제 갈 길 가버리고
안개마저 홀연히 사라져버린
그 끝
거짓말처럼 위병소 말뚝이 우뚝 나타났다.

그러나 차에서 내려서자

the place, again becoming immeasurably distant,
mixed with the fog.

With two men who joined me at the entrance,
we walked and walked, as if being chased,
hurriedly on single concrete path
stretching alongside a long barbed-wire fence
partly revealed to my right in the fog.

At last, a gloomy object appeared,
entered inside,
nothing but cold faces, cold toes,
only the tough connection from this world,
the outside food brought in,
paced about restlessly.

An infinitely long time
to wait for a short encounter.
To kill time, I had to again walk surrounding inside,

I happened to read "How to Rule Myself" on a wall:
.... live with a repenting heart
rather than hating others....

Outside the window
the fog rushed again like the rising tide,
shouting and shrieking.

그곳은 또다시 가늠할 수 없는
거리로 멀어지며
다시금 안개와 뒤섞이고

우측으로 힐끗 드러나는
긴 철책 따라
콘크리트 외길을
때각때각 뚜덕뚜덕
입구에서 합류한 두 사람과 함께
쫓기듯 걷고 또 걸었다.

마침내 우중충한 물체가 드러나고
그 속에는
추운 얼굴, 시린 발끝
사식私食을 넣는 이승에서의 모진 연줄만
서성이고 있었다.

면회를 기다리는
아득히 먼 시간,
그 시간을 죽이려 또다시 제자리걸음으로
또 걸어야 했다.

벽에 걸린 〈나를 다스리는 법〉을 읽었다.
... 남을 미워하기 보다는
    내가 참회하는 마음으로 살아라...

창밖에는
다시금 안개가 밀물져 오며
우우우
아우성을 쳐댔다.

Crossing Taewha Bridge

I still remember
when I was seven years old,
a young man in our village churning
the water to fish out a pig being
carried off by the current, along with a thatched cottage,
after heavy flood.
The Taewha River that comes to mind
is no more the river for fond memories.

Wriggling like the small intestines of a pig,
river water is contaminated, muddy
with over 0.005ppm of heavy metals,
maximum permissible limit of phenol.
It even refuses to reflect
any part of my face.

Some seagulls, having lost their way
while flying along the sea routes,
wander about between
the hazy sky and muddy river.

In Ulsan City, familiar faces are no more,
having scattered in all direction
like flocks of birds. Now the city is crowded

태화교를 건너며

일곱 살 적 큰 물 뒤
초가집과 함께 떠내려가던
돼지를 건지려 동네청년 하나 장대를 휘젓던
기억 불현듯 떠오르는
태화강太和江은 이미 추억의 강이 아니다.

돼지 곱창처럼 꾸무럭거리며
페놀 허용치 0.005ppm 넘어서는
탁한 중금속 물살은 얼비치는
내 얼굴의 편린마저 거부한다.

바닷길 따라 날다
잘못 찾아든 갈매기 몇 마리
흐린 하늘
흐린 강 사이를 방황하고

낯익은 얼굴들이
새떼처럼 흩어져 떠나고 없는 울산엔
악다구니 생존의 터전 찾아 둥지 튼
철새들만 가득하다.

이른 저녁시간에 일어난
시외버스터미널 앞 뺑소니사고
번연히 목격자가 있을 터인데

with only the migratory birds that have built their nests,
searching for bases of survival in a fierce struggle.

Early in the evening one day,
a hit-and-run accident occurred
in front of an intercity bus terminal.
Surely there must be eyewitnesses,
but no one came forth, though the police
appealed to citizens for over a month.
There are no human face.

'Samsan Plain', where green rice plants are dying,
withered yellow by the sooty smoke of factories,
is now prime for the preparation
of large-scale apartment complexes
instead of farming.

I cannot judge whether construction is more
profitable than cultivating rice,
whether men and their children are safe
while rice plants are blighted yellow.
It seems like the hit-and-run case.

By the Taewha River
where we used to bathe in the summer
is an unbroken succession of snack stalls,
inns, and hotels. and
on the corner of an alley

시경에서 한 달을 하소연해도
나타나야할 증인이 없다.
'사람의 얼굴'이 없다.

푸릇한 벼 포기가
공장굴뚝 매연에 누렇게 죽어가는
'삼산평야' 엔 농사 대신 대규모 아파트단지가
들어설 채비로 한창이다.

벼농사보다 사람농사가 수지맞는지,
공해단지에 벼는 누렇게 말라 죽어도
사람과 그 새낀 끄덕도 없는지,
알다가도 모를 일이다.
뺑소니사고와 같이 오리무중이다.

여름이면 멱 감던 태화강변엔
포장마차, 무슨 장莊, 호텔이 즐비하고
골목길 한 켠에선
처녀를 앗긴 처녀가
새벽 3시까지 섧게 울어도
아무도 얼굴을 내미는 이가 없다.

태화강엔
태화교가 가로놓여 있지만
씽씽 매연 뒤꽁무니에 달고
줄행랑치는 버스, 덤프트럭, 뺑소니차는 있어도
태화교를 건너는 사람의 발길은 드물다.

a virgin, robbed of her virginity,
weeps ruefully until three in the morning,
but no face appears from the windows.

Taewha Bridge lies across the river,
there are hit-and-run taxis,
dump trucks, runaway buses,
but it is rare
to find people crossing the bridge.

True natives of Ulsan are found no more,
Those who used to dive in the Taewha River,
were excited to see the circus troupe,
to cross the bridge to watch movie
late night, and afterward, enjoyed
the taste of sweet red-bean soup
at the entrance of Taehwa river.

태화강에서 자맥질하고
서커스단 구경에 설레고
다리 건너 떼 지어
밤늦은 극장 구경을 다녀와
태화강 입구에서 단팥죽 맛을 즐기던
진짜 울산사람은 없다.

Oxen of Halla Mountain, Jeju Island

Frightened by the sound of gunshot
the massacring between men,
the ox hid himself in the mountain
and became an untamed wild ox.

You learned obedience as a virtue,
ruminating on the duties of a servant,
are grateful to be used
as an instrument of men.
However, when you rushed about
madly one day, roaming every where
on the desolate stone mountain,
the village on the far side
was stained with blood, and sea waves
writhed wildly like a wounded animal.

The oxen no longer recognized man as a human,
by hiding themselves in a deeper mountain
to avoid the scent of man,
familiarized themselves with darkness,
and learned an untamed, tough life.

Then, the oxen with no master
joined together,

한라산의 소

총소리에 놀라
인간들끼리의 살육에 놀라
산으로 숨어버린 소는
야생의 들소가 되었다.

순종을 미덕으로 알아
종의 직분을 반추하며
인간의 도구로 쓰임에 감사하던 네가
어느 날 미쳐 날뛰며
황량한 돌산 천방지축 헤매일 때
저 켠 인간의 마을은 피로 물들고
파도는 상채기 난 짐승마냥 뒤챘다.

소는 인간을 더 이상 인간으로 알지 않고
인간의 냄새를 피해
더 깊은 산속으로 숨어들어
어둠을 익히고
야생의 거친 삶을 배웠다.

그리고 임자 없는 저들끼리 어우러져
우우우우우
산울음을 울었다.

잃어버린 소를 찾아 나선 인간이

moo, moo, moo, moo, moo!
Rang out the cries in the mountain.

The men who went to retake their oxen
were struck by enraged horns
laid down on the ground.
Overcome with fright,
they never climbed mountain in search of their oxen.

Even now, on a pitch-black night
from a ridge near the top of Halla Mountain
rise the sounds of oxen herds
can hear disturbing footmarks with burning eyes
like those of wildcat,
The sea waves, frightened by wild oxen's crying
moo, moo, moo, moo, moo!
lie low, very low, cowardly
to the ground.

분노한 소뿔에 되받혀 널브러지고
겁에 질린 그네들은
그후론 다시는 소를 찾아 나서지 않았다.

지금도 캄캄한 밤
한라산 7부 능선쯤에선
살쾡이 같은 밤불 켠 소떼
발자국소리 어지럽고
우우우우우
소 울음소리에 질린 파도는
낮게낮게
뭍에 엎드린다.

Pampas Grass

- On Jeju Island

With what
will your soul be tied down?

Were you unable to keep yourself
the eager longing buried deep in your heart?
Breaking into whiteness,
do you stand still, as if to greet
the hillside and river bank?

The scar of our mean history bloom
as wind flowers scattered here and there,
covering whole my breast,
under the unusually clear sky,
I also see the rusted splinter still stuck painfully
at the top of your feet, cold
and half buried in soil, half soaked in blood.

With what
can your soul be consoled?

Though I embrace you with my bosom,
wide enough to embrace the sky,
rolling about with your lamenting spirit,
how can I amuse your soul to sleep,
that, scattered in the wind,
floats about, without shape,
in the empty space?

억새풀

- 제주도에서

무엇으로
네 넋을 붙들어 매 주랴.

가슴 속 깊이 파묻힌 절절한 그리움
끝내 홀로 간직하지 못하고 허옇게 부서지며
산 둔덕, 강 언덕
마중 나오듯 발길 모두어 섰느냐.

비루한 역사의 상흔
오늘 분분히 흩날리는 바람꽃으로 피어나
내 가슴 가득히 뒤덮고
유난히도 맑은 하늘 아래
반쯤은 흙을,
반쯤은 피를 머금은
네 시린 발등에
아직도 아리게 박혀있는
녹슨 파편이 함께 보이는구나.

무엇으로
네 혼을 위로해 주랴.

하늘을 품고도 남을 내 가슴으로
한 아름 보듬고 뒹굴어도
바람으로 흩어져
형해도 없이 허공에 떠도는
네 넋
내 어찌 잠재울 수 있으랴.

Silence of God

Though there may be no God,
the study of God will be necessary.

Even in the 21st century when logic makes logic,
only religion is unchanged, all-knowing,
omnipotent beyond logic,
and flies from earth to eternity.

The alchemy that even transforms death
into the blessing of life.

If the first quotation that deduced logic
was wrong, how can the contradiction
contained in the logic be proved retroactively?
The yoke of mankind cannot free itself from
being pressed down by the weight of history,
which has been piled layer upon layer
as dense as the thickness of the sins
committed by the human race.

In the beginning, God Almighty created
heaven and earth with His word.
However, if that God had put the vast yoke
somewhere outside the ozone layer of earth
in order to separate the heavenly kingdom
from this earth that is falling into a black hole
of all kinds of inconsistencies and massacres,

신의 침묵

설령 신이 없다 할지라도 신학의 연구는 필요할 것이다.

논리가 논리를 만드는 21세기에도
종교만은 변함없이 논리를 뛰어넘어 전지전능
지상에서 영원으로 날아다닌다.

죽음을 삶의 축복으로까지 탈바꿈시키는 연금술.

만약 논리를 이끌어내는 최초의 인용문이 잘못 되었을 때
그 논리가 갖는 모순을 어떻게 거슬러 입증할 수 있을까?
인류가 저지른 죄의 두께만큼
켜를 이뤄 쌓이고 쌓인 역사의 무게에 짓눌려
헤어나지 못하는 인간의 굴레.

태초에 말씀으로 천지를 창조하신 위대한 하나님.
그 하나님이 온갖 모순과 살육,
증오와 자가당착의 블랙홀로 빠져드는
이 지상과 하늘나라를 차단하고자 지구 오존층 밖 어디쯤
거창한 굴레를 씌운 채 기나긴 잠에 빠져 계신다면,
독생자 예수를 보내도
도무지 구원의 싹이 보이지 않는
인간들에게 절망해버리셨다면
혹여
선한 하나님이 인간들이 하늘나라까지 오염시킨

of hatred and self-contradiction,
if He despaired of men who showed
no possibility of being saved,
though He sent Jesus, His only Son,
or, if that good God were totally exhausted
in the tiresome war with the devils
who polluted even the heavenly kingdom
and so kept consistently "the silence of God,"
what kind of meaning should we understand,
for the word of the beginning of the world?

In this age of confusion
when God no longer condemns the wrongdoing of humanity,
no more with the Noah's Flood,
no more miracle of Jesus happened two thousand years ago
and the prophet's word
is not delivered with its true meaning,
numerous false messengers become witness
with sugarcoated words.

The age overflowing full of grace by words
indulgences and blessings are put on sale
for good but frail people
who still foolishly tremble for fear of the epigram
in the age of Genesis, the Old Testament,
saying that any uncircumcised man would die
and have no child to succeed him.

Annoying hot and humid weather is overlapping
the boring rainy season, even today.

악령들과의 고단한 싸움에
심신이 지칠 대로 지쳐서
'신의 침묵'으로 일관하고 계신다면
그 태초의 말씀은 어떠한 의미로 받아들여야 할까.

하나님이 더 이상 노아의 홍수로
잘못된 인류를 정죄하지 않고
2000년 전 예수의 기적도 재현하지 않고
말씀이 말씀으로 제대로 전달되지 않는 이 혼효의 시대에
한 무리 거짓 선지자들이
말씀에 당의정糖衣錠을 발라 증언하고 있다.

아직도 할례割禮받지 않은 자는
대가 끊기고 죽음에 이른다는
창세기 구약 경구에 벌벌 떠는
선량하고 섬약한 자들에게
면죄부와 복을 동시에 세일하는
은혜 충만 말씀의 홍수시대

오늘 하루도 짜증나는 무더위와 지루한 장마가 겹친다.

Open Space and Open Heart

by Kwon Doowhan
Professor of Korean Literature, Seoul National University

Shin Kee-Sup's poetry looks frank and clear. Nevertheless, this does not mean that his poems are plain. As all poetry should pursue by nature, his poems feel close to us, and as a result, provide us with extraordinary impression and enjoyment - by no means common.

Most remarkable thing in his poems would be his sight and interest towards nature and it focused on what reflects in the poet himself rather than physical figure of nature.

However, when he observes, confronts scenes where men destroy and abuse the nature with whom he resides so steadfast and dear, his concerns change abruptly. He censures self-deteriorated humanity and lack of harmony with nature, and furthermore predicts a horrible future where nature mistreated and damaged by men, attacks and destroys humankind in adverse.

The image of rebellious cows that had once accepted obedience to men as a virtue in 'Oxen of Halla Mountain' reminded me of the movie, 'The Birds' directed by Alfred

열린 공간, 열린 마음의 시

권두환 / 서울대학교 국문과 교수

신기섭의 시는 솔직하고 담백하다. 그렇다고 해서 그의 시가 평범하기만 하다는 이야기는 결코 아니다. 그의 시는, 시가 원래 그러해야만 하는 것처럼, 우리 가까이 자리하면서 결코 평범하지 않은 감동과 감흥을 자아내고 있다.

신기섭의 자연을 읊은 시를 통하여, 우리는 시인이 대상을 바라보는 시선과 관심이 어디를 향해 어떻게 열려 있는가를 확인할 수 있다. 가장 먼저 눈에 띄는 것은 시인이 자연을 바라보되 그 시선과 관심이 자기 자신의 내면을 향해 있는 경우다.

그러나 그 미덥고 친근하던 자연이 인간에 의해 훼손되고 파괴되는 현장을 목격할 때 시인의 시선과 관심은 갑작스러울 정도로 변한다.

그러한 자연의 부조화와 더불어 파괴되어 가는 인간성을 고발하고 있다. 그러한 또 하나의 인식은 인간에 의해 파괴된 자연이 역으로 인간을 공격하고 파괴하는 상황까지를 예감하고 있다.

이 작품은 히치콕 감독의 〈새〉를 연상하게 하는 면이 없지 않

Hitchcock.

This poem symbolizes man's inner being, or humanity as a whole, rather than nature. Lines such as "The oxen no longer recognized man as human being" are indicative of this symbolic intent. Thus, while the poem strongly warns us of nature's aggressions towards men, it also urges the recovery of "lost cows" and "destroyed humanity." His poems about nature naturally concern the simultaneous recovery of nature and human being.

Though he may sound critical or fervent when addressing the subject of nature, these views and concerns are similarly revealed when he writes about men from his overseas experiences or modern history. His voice, moreover, is filled with a deep love for those men who are alienated from common society.

For Shin Kee-sup, poetry functions hope and salvation that is open not only to the poet, but also to all men who live in a so-called industrialized society. I may dare to say that poet Shin's hope and salvation should be deserved more precious as those are the valuable products rooted on his unique worldwide careers and experience.

It is this poet's firm belief that all people's mind in this world should be opened towards the truth. The sincerity with which the poet lives his everyday life, the passion reflected in his works, and his belief in salvation extracted from nature and by elevating human mind are ardently expressed in his piece, "The Door."

다. 인간에 대한 순응을 미덕으로 삼아 오던 소의 반란이 그런 연상을 가능하게 한다. 그러나 이 작품의 소는 자연을 대변한다기보다는 인간의 내면 즉 인간성을 상징하고 있다. '소들이 더이상 인간을 복종해야 할 인간으로 인식하지 않는' 등의 구절이 그런 상징성을 잘 말해 주고 있다. 다시 말하면 이 작품은 인간을 향한 자연의 분노에 대하여 강하게 경고하고 있는 한편, '잃어버린 소' 즉 '파괴된 인간성'의 회복이 시급하다는 사실을 아울러 말하고 있는 것이다.

따라서 그의 자연을 읊은 시는 자연스럽게 자연과 인간의 동시적 회복이라는 주제를 겨냥하게 된다.

그의 시가 지니는 이러한 시선과 관심은 인간을 읊은 시, 해외 체험을 바탕으로 한 시, 역사를 읊은 시에서도 그대로 드러난다. 다만 그 목소리가 좀 더 비판적이고 강한 어조를 띠고 있을 뿐이다. 이들 시편들이 대부분 보통사람들로부터 소외된 사람들에 대한 깊은 애정을 담고 있는 것이 이 때문이다.

그에게 있어서 시는 희망이자 구원인 것이다. 그 희망과 구원은 시인 자신에게는 물론 이른 바 산업사회를 살아가는 모든 사람들을 향해 열려있는 것이라고 할 것이다. 이것은 신기섭 시인이 남다른 이력으로부터 얻은 체험을 바탕으로 한 것이기에 더욱 값진 것이라고 할 만하다.

이 세상의 모든 마음은 진실을 향해 열려야만 한다는 것이 이 시인의 신념이라고 할 수 있다. 신기섭 시인의 생활에 대한 성실성, 일에 대한 열정, 자연을 통한 그리고 인간 정신의 고양을 통한 구원 가능성에 대한 믿음 등등이 '문'이라는 한 편의 시에 절절하게 토로되고 있다고 할 것이다.

Tremor of One's Being

by Choi Shihan
Novelist & Professor of Korean Literature, Sookmyung Women's University

Among the poems included in this book, I think the pieces to reveal poet Shin's mental and spiritual state are those that treat nature as the subject for his pure imagination.

In this poetry book, however, the poet often does not transparently reveal the distinctions between self and nature. Instead, something boils up from within the self and envelops nature, thereby absorbing nature into the self and, from the resultant tremors, sends out emotion and meanings like electronic transmission. In these instances, nature is not simply nature, but an object that is acquired by himself.

This poetry book also includes compositions that are different from those mentioned above. These poems are based on the poet's critical views of reality. These, so to speak, show that the poetic self has been tinged with social consciousness, and therefore, it is characterized

신기섭의 시 세계

존재의 떨림

최시한 / 소설가·숙명여자대학교 국문과 교수

여기 수록된 시들 가운데 필자가 보기에 신기섭 시인의 정서적 원형을 보여주는 것은 자연을 대상으로 순수한 상상을 펼치는 작품들이다.

그런데 이 시집에서 시인은 이와 같이 자아와 사물이 구별되지 않는, 떨림 그대로의 투명한 토로를 자주 보여주지 않는다. 그보다 자아 속에서 끓어오르는 무엇이 자연을 덮으면서, 말하자면 자연이 자아 속으로 빨려 들어와 자아의 떨림에 따라 어떤 느낌과 의미를 전파처럼 쏘는 경우가 많다. 이 때 자연은 자연이라기보다 자아에게 포착된 하나의 '사물' 이다.

이 시집에는 앞에서 살핀 작품들과는 다소 다른 갈래의 시들이 있다. 앞의 작품들이 자아와 자연 혹은 사물의 만남에서 비롯된 것이라면, 이들은 현실에 대한 자아의 비판적 발언에 바탕을 두고 있다. 말하자면 이 작품들은 시적 자아의 정체가 사회성이 짙어서 그의 정서 또한 보편적 존재 현실보다 특정한

by more masculine emotion and social realities than the pure self and the realities of universal existence.

These poems, which are more concrete than other compositions, are clearly distinct from general lyric poems. Therefore, they can be seen as pursuing something new while foregoing something that other poems include. The something foregone is the expression of the inner side. The something new is social criticism in "here and now!"

The book written by Poet Shin reveals a broad scope and great variety of themes from the mind of poet with passion for his homeland, religious awakening, and the realities of international society. His method of expression is meditative and resolute. The form of his compositions is quite free.

Though these poems are of a different kind, a certain vibe can be felt through them. This vibe is tinged with purposeful responsibility and ethics rather than romantic or transcendental colors. The social criticism that has been incorporated, moreover, looks broad and deep. While this largely stems from the poet's singular experiences and concerns in various countries, it is nonetheless an uncommon quality in Korea's poetical circles where narrowly defined lyrical poems are abundant.

사회현실에 대한 보다 남성적인 정서가 두드러진 시들이다.

목소리가 다른 어떤 시들보다도 단호하고 구체적인 이런 작품들은 분명 일반적인 서정시하고는 거리가 있다. 그러므로 다른 시들이 지닌 무엇인가를 밀어놓고 대신 다른 것을 추구했다고 볼 수 있다. 그 밀어놓은 것이란 사물과의 만남을 통한 내면의 표현이고, 대신 추구한 것이란 '지금 여기'에서의 사회비판이다.

신기섭 시인의 이번 시집은 격정을 품은 개인의 내면에서부터 고향 풍경, 종교적 각성을 거쳐 격렬하게 싸우는 국제사회의 현실에 이르기까지 그 제재의 폭이 매우 넓고 다채롭다. 그리고 어법이 사색적이고 단호하고 형식도 매우 자유롭다.

갈래는 다르지만 이런 시들에서도 여전히 떨림은 느껴진다. 그 떨림은 낭만적이거나 초월적인 색채 대신 책임과 윤리의 의지적 색채를 띠고 있다. 그리고 이들에 담긴 사회적 비판은 매우 넓고 깊다. 분명히 시인의 여러 나라에 걸친 체험과 관심 때문일 터인데 이는 좁은 의미에서의 '서정시'가 많은 한국 시단에서 흔하지 않은 예이다.

Poetry Book Introduction

by Kwon Tae-kyun,
Ambassador of Republic of Korea to UAE

The publication of the English-Korean poetry book Rose Stone in Arabian Sand by Mr. Shin Ki-sup, Vice President of Dohwa Engineering, is a truly meaningful occasion. As a construction engineering expert, the poet has amassed a wealth of knowledge on the history and culture of Islamic countries while living in Saudi Arabia, Oman, Bahrain, UAE in the Arabian Peninsula, and Indonesia for the past 10 years. He is also a veteran among Korean poets and his work "After Being Embraced by the Mountain" adorns the doors of one of the most crowded subway stations in the center of Seoul.

While serving as Ambassador of the Republic of Korea to the UAE for the past 3 years, I have heard countless poems recited at events and felt the Arab people's affection towards poetry. Based on these experiences, I was especially delighted and proud to learn that this rare collection of poems, which reflects the unique beauty of the desert, the humanity and compassion of the Islamic

시집 소개

권태균 / 주 아랍에미리트 대사

도화엔지니어링 신기섭 부사장이 출간한 'Rose Stone in Arabian Sand' 영한시집은 참으로 의미있게 여겨집니다.

시인은 건설 엔지니어링 전문가로서 지난 10년간 아라비아 반도 사우디아라비아, 오만, 바레인, UAE와 인도네시아에 거주하면서 이슬람국가의 역사와 문화에 대해 많은 경험과 지식을 습득하였습니다. 뿐만 아니라 그는 서울 시내 가장 번화한 지하철역 스크린도어에 '산의 품에 든 후' 라는 시가 게재된 중견시인입니다.

지난 3년간 UAE 한국대사로서 UAE에서 활동하면서, 저는 여러 중요한 행사에서 시가 낭송되는 것을 보고 시에 대한 아랍인들의 강한 애정을 목격해 왔습니다. 이러한 경험에 비춰 볼 때 사막에 대한 독특한 미학을 묘사하고 이슬람인들에 대해 인간적인 교감, 열사의 외진 건설현장에서 겪는 한국근로자들의 기쁨과 슬픔을 묘사한, 아주 보기 드문 시들을 접하고 이러한 시들이 한국인에 의해 쓰여졌다는 데 특별한 기쁨과 자

people, and the joys and sorrows felt by foreign workers at isolated project sites, was written by a fellow Korean.

I believe that this book will promote interaction and friendly relations between the people of the Middle East and the Republic of Korea. Moreover, I hope the poems contained in this book will be able to convey the essence of Korean culture to foreign societies.

랑스러움을 느낍니다.

저는 이 시집을 통해 중동사람들과 한국인 사이에 교감이 이루어져 상호간의 유대관계가 한층 촉진되고 발전해 나가리라 믿어 의심치 않습니다.

한 걸음 더 나아가 저는 이 시집에 나오는 독창적인 시들이 한국 전통문화의 진수를 아랍 사회에 전하는 계기가 될 것을 희망합니다.

Congratulatory Remark

by Chung Ki-Jong,
Ambassador of the Republic of Korea to Qatar

By reading the poems of Shin Kee-Sup, we are able to know the Middle East's Key Words such as rose stone, desert, Palestinian friend, and Bedouin are not only representative of that part of the world, but reveal a compassion, respect, and love for Arabic history, culture and spirituality.

I imagine it would be difficult for any man not to lose his will and ability to compose literary works after entering the corporate world. Moreover, maintaining one's sense of poetic expression in an Arabic country where the climate and social environment are completely dissimilar to those of one's homeland would be an even greater challenge. In that regard, Shin Kee-sup is surely to a man whose pure heart and artistic abilities are unique.

Everyone who visits Qatar is astonished by the drastically changed appearance of this rapidly evolving state. One can admire the splendid nightline of Doha, a city full

404 Congratulatory Remark

축사

정기종 / 주 카타르대사

신기섭 시인의 시를 읽으면 여러 가지 중동의 키워드가 담겨 있음을 알 수 있습니다.

장미석, 사막, 팔레스타인 친구, 베두윈 등과 같은 단어들과 여기서 시작되는 감정의 이입은 아랍의 역사와 문화, 정신세계에 대한 경의와 애정이 담겨 있다고 보여 집니다.

학창시절 이후 사회에 진출하여 직장생활을 하면서도 문학을 하는 정신을 잃지 않기는 쉽지 않은 일이라고 생각합니다. 더구나 기후와 사회 환경이 우리와는 매우 다른 중동아랍국에 살아가면서 이러한 시심을 간직하고, 그것을 글로 표현하기는 더더욱 어려운 일이라고 할 것입니다.

신기섭 시인은 이런 면에서 보통사람과 다른 순수한 마음과 특별한 능력을 가지고 있는 분임에 틀림없다 할 것입니다.

카타르를 방문하는 사람들은 누구나 놀랍게 발전한 도시의 모습에 놀라게 됩니다. 세계적인 유명 건축가들이 지은 초현

of modern buildings designed by the world's foremost architects, and savor the emerald waves of the West Bay from the coffee shop of the Islam Museum.

However, we cannot truly understand Qatar from the state's outward appearance, and without genuine understanding, it is difficult to achieve cooperation with the people of Qatar. Mutual cooperation can only be realized after we understand and empathize with the history, culture and faith that are close to their hearts.

In this context, I believe Shin Kee-sup's activities as a poet and the fruits of his efforts are deeply meaningful not only for his personal journey in life, but also for relations between both countries. Once again, I congratulate the publication of his poetry collection and pray for his good health as well.

대식 건축물이 가득한 도하시내의 화려한 야경에 경탄하게 되고, 이슬람 박물관의 커피숍에 앉아 에메랄드빛 바닷물 너머 보이는 웨스트 베이의 풍경을 음미할 수 있는 즐거움도 만끽할 수 있는 것입니다.

그러나 단지 이러한 외연적인 면만을 보고 카타르를 이해한다고 할 수 없겠으며, 더구나 카타르인들과의 협력을 이끌어내기는 어렵습니다. 이들의 마음에 새겨진 역사와 문화 그리고 신앙을 이해하고 공감할 수 있어야 어떤 협력도 함께 할 수 있다고 할 것입니다.

이러한 면에서 신기섭 시인의 시작활동과 그 결실인 시작품은 개인적인 인생의 여정에서뿐만 아니라 양국의 민간외교 활동에서도 매우 의미가 깊은 일이라고 믿어집니다. 다시 한번 시집 발간을 축하드리며 더욱 건승하시기를 기원합니다.

A Thought on
'Rose Stone in Arabian Sand'

Fernandes Hilary Anthony,
Coordinator Woongjin Development Co. LLC Oman)
-from Goa, India. B.Sc Bombai Univ. He has been working in Middle East 40 years since 1975.

The poetry collection 'Rose Stone in Arabian Sand' by
Shin Kee-sup is a record of the poet's actual experiences
while working and living in the Middle East and Indonesia. To many, poetry is a form of writing that is often
misconstrued and difficult to understand. It is, however,
arguably the purest form of writing, a form characterized
by the beauty of love expressed through language. It is
an art, and as an expression of what the poet thinks and
feels, it is very difficult to define. It can take any form
that the writer chooses. In general, it is an expression for
the purpose of stirring up an emotion in the audience and
holding them spellbound.

As I read through this poetry collection, I found myself
imagining the writer's perspective on living in the
Middle East, which is a predominantly Muslim world,
and Indonesia, a Southeast Asian Muslim country with
a very different culture. Then, as he carried his thoughts
and experiences back to his home country and the

'Rose stone in Arabian Sand'에 대한 견해

Hilary Fernandes
웅진개발(Offshore 중동진출 한국회사) Project Coordinator
봄베이대학교 Science전공, 1975년 이후 중동 40년 경력.

신기섭 박사의 영한시집 'Song from the Arabian Sand'는 시인인 저자가 중동지역과 인도네시아에서 살면서 실제 일을 하면서 관찰한 실제경험과 지역 사회생활이 결합된 체험적 기록물로 보여진다.

시는 오늘날에도 여전히 논란의 여지를 남기는 쉽게 이해하기 어려운 영역이나, 한편으로 언어를 통해 표현할 수 있는 사랑의 아름다움으로 특징지어지는 미적인 영역에서 가장 순수한 특성을 지니고 있기도 하다. 또한 예술의 한 분야로서의 시는 시인 스스로가 생각하고 느낀 부분을 표현함에 있어 그가 원하는 형식을 선택하기 때문에 정확히 규정짓기가 상당히 어려운 면이 있다. 일반적으로 시인은 그의 상상력을 동원해 독자들의 감정을 흔들어 사로잡으려는 시도를 한다.

'Rose stone in Arabian Sand' 제목으로 엮은 시들에서 중동지역에서는 이슬람이 절대적 가치로 지배하는 아랍인의 삶에 얽힌 체험적 삶에 대한 작가의 생각을 읽을 수 있었다.

인도네시아동남아시아는 중동과 같은 이슬람권이나 문화적으

collective imagination of his people, his wish to harmonize his own thoughts with the concrete world was most interesting.

I am thankful for having known Dr. Shin for over six years. Having worked with him in Muscat and Salalah in Oman, and also in Abu Dhabi where his principal company was engaged in offshore construction projects, I found him to be a compassionate, educated and knowledgeable man in a company of multinationals. His cool and composed personality helped him get along with people of varied cultural backgrounds. I personally treasure the memories I have of working and living with him, and I hope that he continues to publish similar works in the near future.

Fernandes Hilary Anthony, Coordinator Woongjin Development Co. LLC Oman)
-from Goa, India. B.Sc Bombai Univ. He has been working in Middle East 40 years since 1975.

로 매우 차이가 나는 가운데 작가의 조국인 한국인을 인도네시아인에게 이입시키는 과정을 살펴볼 수 있었다. 이 두 국가 간의 일치된 세계가 작가 자신만의 개성있는 생각을 통해 창의적으로 이미지화시키고 혼연일체가 되어 있어 내게 너무나 흥미롭게 느껴졌다.

나는 신박사가 근무한 해상 건설프로젝트 건설회사에서 6년 이상 오만 살랄라와 무스캇 그리고 UAE 아부다비에서 그를 보필하면서 개인적으로 아주 가까이서 그를 접하며 알 수 있는 기회를 가진 것을 기쁘게 생각하고 있다.

그는 다국적인들이 모인 회사에서 인간적인 이해심, 풍부한 지식과 지혜로움으로 직원들을 완벽하리만큼 잘 이끌어나갔다. 그의 차분하고 조직적인 소양이 다양한 문화배경을 지닌 사람들과 쉽게 화합해 나가는 데 도움을 주었다.

내 자신은 개인적으로 신박사와 지근거리에서 함께 살고 일한 기억을 보석같이 소중히 간직하고 있다. 그가 가까운 장래에 또 다른 좋은 작품을 출간할 수 있기를 희망한다.

His Poem Pursues Our Life's Ultimate Goal: To Be One (with God)

by Gazi Darici, Turkey
Managing Partner,
MSCE(Master of Science, Civil Engineering)
KULAK Construction Co. Abu Dhabi, UAE

Life is a kind of poem; sometimes harmonious like the rhythm a poem contains within itself, and sometimes inharmonious like how reality is.

However, while there is (full stop) in a poem, life is forever in that we live to be part of 'The One' after death and 'to be One' in a broader sense. 'The One' is God, I believe... This kind of meaningful metaphor is reflected in the passionate, symbolic poems of 'Rose Stone in Arabian Sand'.

At the same time, I firmly believe that working hard, as the most valuable virtue in this world, is a means of dedicating oneself to God. Recognized worldwide as hard workers, the Korean and Turkish people have become prosperous by overcoming their desperate fates from the ashes of war and ruined empires.

The various emotional and thoughtful colors (poems)

신기섭 시인의 열정적인 시는
인간이 추구해야 할 완성된 인간,
즉 신을 향해 있다

가지 다르즈, Kulak Construction Co. UAE 대표
Master Engineer, Turkey

인생은 시가 지닌 운율이 있어 조화로운 면이 있으나, 때로는 현실에서 드러나는 그대로 부조화로운 면에 있다는 점에서 시와 유사하다는 생각을 지니고 있습니다.

그러나 시의 형식은 예외 없이 마침표로 끝맺게 되나, 인생은 죽음 이후에 더 큰 하나신의 일부가 되고 궁극적으로 큰 하나신적인 존재로 승화된다는 점에서 차이점이 있다고 저는 믿고 있습니다.

이런 의미에서 신기섭 시인의 열정과 상징적 의미가 담긴 시 '아라비아사막의 장미석Rose Stone in Arabian Sand' 는 개체로서의 인간이 더 큰 통합된 하나신적인 존재로 나아가는 데 궁극적인 가치가 있다고 봅니다.

평소에 제 자신은 '일을 열심히 하는 것' 이야말로 이 세상에서 가장 가치 있는 덕목으로서 '자신을 신에게 봉헌하는 것'

that bloom in a poet's inner mind are great gifts for humankind and worthy of being dedicated to 'The One'. Many thanks to Dr. Shin for reminding us of this truth with his lovely poems.

이라는 신념을 지니고 있습니다. 일을 열심히 하는 민족으로 전 세계에 널리 알려진 한국인과 터키인은 패망한 왕국과 전쟁의 잿더미라는 절망적인 운명을 극복하고 오늘의 번영을 이룩해 나가는 공통점이 있습니다.

신기섭 시인 내면에서 꽃피우는 다양한 열정적이고 사색적인 색깔을 띤 시들은 인간에게 주는 위대한 선물이며 신에게 바칠 만한 가치있는 작품으로 생각됩니다.

그의 사랑스런 시들을 통해 이러한 진리를 일깨워준 신박사에게 고마움을 전합니다.